Camelback Falls

Books by Jon Talton

The David Mapstone Mysteries
Concrete Desert
Camelback Falls
Dry Heat
Arizona Dreams
Cactus Heart

Other Novels
The Pain Nurse

Camelback Falls

Jon Talton

Poisoned Pen Press

Copyright © 2003 by Jon Talton

First Paperback Edition 2009

10 9 8 7 6 5 4 3 2 1

Library of Congress Catalog Card Number: 2008937725

ISBN: 978-1-59058-644-0 Trade Paperback

Poisoned Pen Press
6962 E. First Ave., Ste. 103
Scottsdale, AZ 85251
www.poisonedpenpress.com
info@poisonedpenpress.com

Printed in the United States of America

*For Susan, as always, and
for my mother, Vivian, who
never stopped loving Phoenix*

Chapter One

We wore our uniforms the day Mike Peralta was sworn in as sheriff of Maricopa County. It nearly made me late to the ceremony.

In the quiet of my forgotten office in the old county courthouse, behind the plastic doorplate that reads "Deputy David Mapstone, Sheriff's Office Historian," I fiddled with the tribal fashion of cops. The tan uniform blouse with epaulets and pocket flaps, the opening above the pocket made for a cheap Cross pen, and the gold-plated "MCSO" letters running parallel on each side of the collar. In one of his moments of cruel whimsy, Peralta gave me two gold book pins for my collar. I refused to wear them.

The shirt had a reinforced grommet to hold a badge. I slipped my gold star out of its wallet case, gave it a last polish, and pinned it on. The five-pointed star proclaimed me "Deputy Sheriff... Maricopa County," on scrolls cut into the metal surrounding the Arizona state seal. *Ditat Deus*, the seal says: God enriches. The ACLU is suing to have the words removed.

Dark brown uniform slacks were pressed crisply, and the legs draped to a slight break over the hand-tooled leather cowboy boots, glistening with a regulation spit shine. An off-white felt Stetson sat on my desk. We might be one of the largest urban counties in the United States, but we kept our Old West traditions.

Finally, I pulled on the heavy belt, also highly polished, that held handcuffs, flashlight loop, Mace canister, keyring,

Speedloaders, and the holster that housed my Colt Python .357 revolver. I loudly snapped the leather keepers that held the gunbelt to the pants belt. Ready at last.

I usually dressed like a civilian, although I liked nice clothes more than the average Arizonan and way more than my paycheck could handle. But that day I stood before the mirror and looked something like the young deputy I had been twenty-three years before, when I was a rookie, out on the street for the first time with a veteran named Peralta. I'm six-foot-two and broadshouldered, with wavy dark hair that goes any way it chooses. Lindsey likes my brown eyes. They don't look like cop's eyes, she says. But that day everything else about me looked cop. I tilted the Stetson at a slight angle and locked up the office.

Outside, the miracle of a winter day in Arizona. The palm trees and paloverdes lining Cesar Chavez Plaza sat lush and spring green. The spare modern towers of downtown Phoenix looked puny under the bright blue firmament of dry desert sky. It was nearly perfect: You could barely see some pockets of yellowbrown smog skulking up against the rocky head of Camelback Mountain. The temperature was in the sweet zone of the seventies. Tourists paid high-season prices for days like this.

I crossed Jefferson Street and went through the metal detectors into the County Supervisors Auditorium. Then I saw no way to get to my seat but to cross the stage, shaking hands with the cluster of family and friends of the new sheriff. Sharon Peralta looked ten years younger in a stylish navy pinstripe suit, her shoulder-length hair expensively done. She'd taken a rare morning off from her radio show to be here at her husband's big day. She smiled to see me in uniform. Their daughters, Jamie and Jennifer, lived in the Bay Area and practiced law. I remembered when they were babies, and I didn't feel old. Judge Peralta, Mike's father, courtly and ancient, grasped my hand strongly in both of his and held me before him for a long time, saying nothing. For just a moment, I felt a strange flutter below my breastbone.

Peralta himself had yet to make his entrance. I shook hands with the department brass, most of them not so sure why I should even be up there. Bill Davidson looked, as always, like the Marlboro Man, tall and craggy with a lush mustache turning steel gray. He was the longtime patrol boss. Jack Abernathy, short legs attached to a beer-barrel chest, was in charge of what was now called "the custody bureau"—the county jail. Both wanted to be chief deputy now that Peralta was in the top job. E.J. Kimbrough, his head shaved like an ebony bullet, clapped me on the arm. He was the captain of the major crimes unit, and he was an ally, maybe a friend. I hoped Peralta would make him the new chief of sheriff's detectives. Last, the outgoing sheriff, controversial and wildly popular. He brought back chain gangs and housed inmates in tents. I'd been a little part of his show. Now he was off to Washington as the new administration's drug czar.

"The history professor," he said, his tone ambiguous, his icy gray eyes unmoving.

I passed the color guard of Boy Scouts and took my place at the end of the stage, where Deputy Lindsey Faith Adams had saved a chair for me. Lindsey favored black miniskirts or jeans. But today, she too wore MCSO tan, her straight black hair parted in the middle and pulled back demurely, her small gold nose stud nowhere to be seen. Even so, Lindsey didn't look like a cop. And if she weren't the star of the cybercrimes task force, she'd probably be making big bucks at a dot-com company. She gave my hand a discreet squeeze. I squeezed back and felt the engagement ring I had given her three months before.

It was 11 A.M. on the second Monday of January.

"So, Mapstone, you ready to take a real job in this department?"

I had to lean over to hear Peralta. The well-worn gymnasium at Immaculate Heart Church must have been filled with a thousand people, all there to wish the new sheriff well. A line of them was snaked around us. The governor, the county supervisors, and the mayor of Phoenix had already come through. But I bet another hundred were lined up behind me. I noticed a bigwig from Phelps Dodge, the managing editor of the *Republic*, the head of the Phoenix Symphony board. Peralta held me by the arm in a nearly painful grip and repeated his question.

"How about it? Are you ready to take a real job in the department?"

"I like what I'm doing, but you could give me more money," I said.

"I'll ask the new sheriff about it," he said. "I'm sure we could get you an off-duty gig as a security guard at Bashas'."

He didn't smile. He never smiled. But he looked happy today. As happy as he could look. Peralta had the surprising bulk of a Victorian armoire. He stood six-foot-five, and if he could have fit into a 48-long coat I would have been surprised. Little of his bulk appeared to be fat. His broad, brown face carried the same impassive expression as always. But his large eyes, where all his emotions congregated, held a little gleam, just like the light hitting the four stars freshly pinned on his uniform collar.

Peralta had spent a quarter century in the department. When I left to go teach college history, he stayed as a sergeant and a comer. During the years I was gone, we stayed in touch as he rose to lieutenant and captain, and I wrote a history book that may have sold a few hundred copies. He had been chief deputy so long that the words "Chief" and "Peralta" seemed inextricably linked. And three years ago, when I failed to get tenure and came home unemployed and more than a little broken, the chief gave me a job in the department researching old unsolved cases. I worked as a consultant, using the historian's techniques but also carrying a badge. I got $1,000 for every case I cracked.

He snorted to himself, breaking me out of my reverie.

"Hell," he said. "I may make you the new chief deputy."

"I'm not qualified." I laughed.

"I did the job for ten years," he said above the din. "I'll decide who's qualified. That'd frost these fucking climbers." He nodded toward a small cluster of brass standing uncomfortably over by the refreshment table.

I tried to change the subject. "This is a great place for the reception."

"I know you'd rather be drinking martinis at the Phoenician," he said. "But this is a sentimental thing."

"You, sentimental? When we were deputies together I had to remind you to get Sharon a card for your anniversary."

His glare hardened. I was one of the few people who dared mess with him.

He said, "I went to first and second grade here, before they had to close the school. My father went to high school here. Who knows how much longer it will be around before your yuppie friends gentrify the neighborhood?"

He added, "And holding the reception here is not a bad way to shore up my support with the Latino voters." He arched his eyebrow, a gesture of enormous humor for him. "I'm just a simple boy from the barrio."

"You're about as simple as quantum physics," I said. I nodded toward the people waiting behind me. "You have lots of VIPs who want to congratulate you, Sheriff,"

He ignored me. "See, Mapstone, I know you. You can't revise your past with me like some professor's résumé. You always should have stayed in law enforcement. So you took a fifteen-year detour as a teacher? Now you're back in Arizona, back home at the S.O. Where you always should have stayed. Even if you're a pain in the ass sometimes and you read too much. Admit it, Mapstone, you're happy here."

He was right. The "black dog moods," as Churchill called them, came less often. I was teaching myself that tomorrow's misfortune wasn't an inevitable byproduct of today's happiness. Lindsey made me feel terrifically lucky. The turn of a new millennium had come and gone benignly, as had my twenty-fifth high school reunion. I was even feeling better about Phoenix, a place that could break your heart if you grew to love it.

The noise picked up, with a mariachi band and the sheriff's office bagpipers engaging in a merry duel.

"But we need to make some changes in the department," he said.

"People may not like it. And I'm serious when I say I expect you to step up when asked."

"Yeah, security at Bashas'," I said "I can also help carry groceries. I know you'll make all the right changes for the department, Sheriff."

"I'm a lawman, Mapstone," he said. "I'm no politician."

"Well, you did pretty well, then. Getting 70 percent of the vote."

"Oh, hell, I'd just have to break in somebody new as sheriff if I didn't do it myself."

I shook my head, awash with affection for this impossible, stubborn, lionhearted man, and I couldn't suppress a wide smile.

"What the hell are you so giggly about?"

"You," I said. "Never mind."

He let go of my arm. "Come by my office tomorrow. I really do need to talk to you about something."

"A new case?"

He gave his head a half nod, half shake. "Come by. You'll find out."

I nodded, then my eyes went to a small, intense flash in the air above Peralta's left shoulder, and I remember thinking he'd be freshly annoyed that I wasn't looking him in the eye. Only later would I recall two distinct, terrible cracks sounding above the clutter. Suddenly Peralta fell into me heavily and we both crashed backward hard on the floor.

I felt the quick panic of having the air knocked out of me. Something wet shot into my eyes. My back screamed in pain from the weight that quickly sandwiched it with the floor. A woman gasped and called for God's help. As my mind refocused and my lungs refilled, I feared Peralta had suffered a heart attack. Then I saw the blood all over us.

Chapter Two

Lindsey commandeered a patrol car and we sped the mile up Seventh Street to Good Samaritan Hospital. The digital clock on the dash said the trip took four minutes. To my internal clockworks, it felt like about a decade.

"I didn't even hear the shots," she said over the siren. "I got there as soon as I could."

I touched her leg. The buildings and traffic flew by, but in my mind was the image of Peralta bloody and unconscious. Maybe he was dead and the paramedics just had to go through their little show.

"Could you see a shooter?" she asked, slowing suddenly. A minivan meandered through a red light, oblivious to the lights and siren of our onrushing sheriff's cruiser.

"A flash, maybe. That's all." It occurred to me she was trying to distract me, focus me on the job rather than the heap of shallowly breathing, traumatized flesh that was my friend. Did I look distraught? I kept my voice steady.

"We didn't seal the building soon enough," I said. "There was too much chaos. I'm not sure they got the guy."

"Maybe it's not a guy," she said.

Chaos. It was like the thunderstorms in the Arizona high country that begin slowly but can suddenly turn nasty. A tense surprise moved through the crowd around us after Peralta fell. Only after seeing the blood was there something like a collective gasp. I regained my wits with only a mouthful of panic and, as gently as I could with such a big man, I rolled Peralta over on his back, and made sure his airway was open and he was breathing. He was, but he stared emptily and only made a long, exhaling sound, his powerful hand grasping my shirt shyly.

Then Lindsey was there, shielding us, sweeping her arm toward the shooter with her baby Glock 9mm semiautomatic, "ready to rock 'n' roll," as she puts it. But no more shots came. I heard her directing other deputies, heard them running across the old wooden floor toward where the gunfire originated. Somewhere above us. As word spread through the crowded gymnasium, civilians tried to get out while cops tried to take charge or get information. Finally the music stopped. Fragments of the crowd swelled around us, nearly stepping on us, until some Phoenix cops set up a perimeter to keep people back. They let Sharon through after a fuss. TV lights flared behind me. Somebody said the paramedics had arrived.

At Good Sam, I saw the dazzling red fire department ambulance was empty, its rear doors still open. Peralta was already deep inside the vast brightness of the trauma center. City cops and deputies milled around officiously. We parked in a space for emergency vehicles and walked quickly to the automatic doors.

"Gurney!" shouted a red-haired nurse as I walked in. I tried to step aside for this next victim, but the nurse was headed straight for me.

"He's OK," Lindsey said, holding out her hand as if to direct traffic. "He's just a mess." She smiled back at me, her twilight blue eyes calm.

"Chief Peralta," I said, then caught myself. "The sheriff. Where is he?"

Just then Sharon strode past the nurse and hugged me tightly, despite the blood all over my uniform. Lindsey looked at me and flashed something in lover's code.

"You're OK?" Sharon demanded, her voice metallic and a notch louder. I nodded. Her eyes were rimmed red but she wasn't crying.

"Where are the girls?" I asked.

"They left to take the Judge home before the party," she said. "Thank God they weren't there when it happened."

Sharon Peralta holds a doctorate from UCLA and she's a best-selling author. She's made more money the past year than I'll see in my lifetime. She's the most popular radio psychologist on the West Coast, dispensing exquisitely nuanced advice from nine to noon every weekday for the latte-and-whole-grain crowd. But walking toward me she looked just as scared and awkward and at sea as the twenty-five-year-old cop's wife she had been the first time I met her. It lasted just a minute.

"They won't even let me in," she said. "He's in emergency surgery." We moved by instinct into an otherwise deserted waiting room. Sharon sat on a greenish sofa, me and Lindsey on either side.

"Oh, David, I thought I didn't have to worry about this anymore. I just thought he'd be a politician now. All those years when he'd go to work and I never knew if he'd…"

We all silently stared at the wall. Sharon said, "God, I still remember that night in Guadalupe, back in 1979, when you and he were patrol deputies. You remember?"

I nodded, recalling a bad shooting years ago. Peralta was a hero. I was scared shitless. If he was, it never showed. I said, "He came out of that just fine, Sharon, and he's going to now."

"Oh, David," she said dully, "you don't have to baby me…" She let the sentence trail off, then something bright and fierce crossed her face. "David, his insulin."

I didn't make the leap with her. She said, "He'll have to have his insulin."

I patted her hand. "Sharon, it's a hospital, they have everything right here."

"David, he's got to have it. It's his prescription. Please. It's in his office refrigerator. Please do this for me." She took a heavy gold key off a ring and handed it out. "This is to his office."

I started to say something, but Lindsey put a hand on my shoulder.

"We'll be here, Dave," she said, looking at me full-on with those incredible blue eyes. "Don't be long."

I gave in to the irrational requests of the terrified and took the key.

A few minutes later, I used the side entrance to the Sheriff's Office headquarters building on Madison Street downtown. I avoided the clots of employees, all awaiting the same news I did. I took the shortcut down an empty corridor where an unmarked door was the back entrance into Peralta's office.

The outgoing sheriff had just moved out of his office that morning, and the county, in the inscrutable wisdom of large bureaucracies, was waiting two weeks to give the place new carpeting, drapes, and paint. So here I was in the familiar room where Chief Deputy Peralta held court all these years. The big desktop was bare and the credenza behind it was piled two feet high with reports. The county seal and Arizona state flag sat photogenically in one corner. An entire wall held photos from Peralta's career. A framed map of the county took up another wall, the yellow urban mass spread ever more into the desert. It was a room where Peralta would sit with his boots up on the desk and philosophize about crime and punishment. Or bark at me, and not affectionately, about the progress on a case. It looked reassuring and familiar, and the events of the past hour were just outside the door.

I squatted before the small refrigerator, and fished past a couple dozen caffeine-free Diet Cokes. I pulled out the insulin bottles and tucked them in my pocket. Peralta had never admitted to me that he had diabetes, and when Sharon told me a couple of years ago I was surprised to realize this invincible man, who seemed incapable of mere human emotions like fear or sentimentality, was as vulnerable as any of us.

I closed up the refrigerator, and as I stood, my eye went to Peralta's beaten-up Franklin Planner, resting precariously on a pile of files. It was open to today, and of course he'd made no notation of the most important event of his career. On the facing page was only one item to do. It read: "Mapstone—Camelback Falls."

Camelback Falls? I made a quick mental list of everything he had me working on: the unsolved disappearance of the minister's wife from 1964; a reassessment of a murder investigation from 1982, because the murderer had been granted a new trial; the Web version of my Sheriff's Office history, which was actually selling well at bookstores in the Valley. I didn't have a clue about "Camelback Falls."

Suddenly, the side door opened and I had company.

It was Jack Abernathy, still in uniform, his bulk stretching at the fabric of the tan shirt. His Charley Tuna face reddened and his mouth crooked down.

"Mapstone, what the hell? What are you doing in here?" His voice was raspy and soft, a Texas drawl poking out on certain words.

He'd never liked me. He was old school Sheriff's Office, where you did your time, kept your mouth shut, and didn't think too much. I failed on all three counts.

"I had to get something for Sharon Peralta. The sheriff is in surgery now."

He stared at me. I said in a steady voice, "What are you doing here?"

He started to speak. Then he turned suddenly and stalked out the door. Under his breath I heard, "Fuck you!"

Chapter Three

I left the commandeered sheriff's cruiser at headquarters to find its way home, and I drove back in Lindsey's old white Honda Prelude. I flipped the radio over to AM, where all the news stations were reporting on the shooting of Sheriff Peralta, just hours after he was sworn in. One newscaster called it an "assassination attempt." "Critical condition" was repeated over and over. Then the station cut to a commercial for Waterworks, a chain of waterbed stores that had somehow survived the 1970s. I felt like an ice spike was lodged in my stomach.

The horrid 1980s tower of Good Sam appeared. It looked like a spaceship from a low-budget science-fiction movie. Outside, the TV satellite trucks were stacked into the parking lot and spilling out onto Twelfth Street. Four reporters, spaced apart like saplings with a wardrobe allowance, were doing live feeds. Inside, cops guarded entrances, patrolled hallways, and stood around looking bored and fingering their gunbelts. After being challenged a half dozen times, I finally returned to the little waiting room where I'd left Lindsey and Sharon. All I wanted was for Peralta to be OK.

He wasn't. He was in a coma.

I sat on a too-comfortable chair as Sharon, now flanked by her daughters, told me what they knew. Two bullets hit Peralta. One entered his back, missed the spine and aorta by no more than an inch, then blew out his chest, fracturing a rib. The second round hit the top of his head. The bullet fragmented, although most of it didn't enter his skull—"His hard old head," Sharon laughed and sniffled. Whether that was lucky enough, nobody knew. They did some exploratory surgery. They did a CAT scan. The chief of neurosurgery was called in, along with a half dozen other specialists from around the city. All they could say was that his brain had been shocked, was under pressure from swelling, and it would take time to know how serious his condition was.

Then, feeling foggy and for the first time sore from where Peralta fell on me, I followed Sharon and Lindsey past more deputies to the ICU.

"They don't know anything" Sharon whispered vehemently, running a hand through her dark hair.

"The doctors?"

"The police," she said.

"They didn't make any arrests?" I demanded.

"No suspects, no motive," Lindsey said. "How could somebody escape from a room with a thousand cops in it?"

Sharon said, "One set of detectives was asking questions about whether it was a hate crime. He's the first Latino sheriff here. Another bunch asked if it could have been a random shooting, that he wasn't the target. Nobody has any answers."

I thought of all the enemies Peralta must have made in his long law enforcement career: drug dealers, skinheads, the Mexican Mafia, the Bloods and Crips, assorted killers and bigtime con artists. I kept it to myself.

Then I was looking through a window at the sheriff. Only his hand was recognizable: that meaty brown fist, with the wedding band still on the ring finger. It still looked formidable. Everything else before us was a mound of gown, covers, tubes, electrodes, monitors, meters, and elaborately joined plastic bags with what looked like whole blood and some kind of IV solution. I felt sick and unreal. I put my arms around Sharon and Lindsey, and we just stood there a long time, saying nothing. A nurse in green scrubs came in and fiddled with some kind of electronic device on the IV line. Finally, Sharon said what we had all been thinking.

"I thought he was indestructible."

‹›‹›‹›

There was nothing to do but sit and wait. We were on hospital time now, something marked by the comings and goings of people in white lab coats and green scrubs, by the traffic of metal carts holding medicine, linens, trays of hospital food, by snippets of TV shows overheard from open rooms, by the occasional scream or cry for help that escapes the carefully orchestrated calm. I had waited like this when my grandparents died. They had raised me after my parents had been lost in a light-plane crash when I was a baby. I had imagined the wait they had for word on their son and daughter-in-law, off to Colorado in a fragile little Cessna. I had no memory of my parents, and yet I carried billions of DNA messages inside me from them. Those messages made me lousy at waiting in hospitals. At 9 P.M., a nurse ran off the non-family members, and we left the Peralta women with hugs and promises to return immediately if anything changed.

Outside the hospital, it was just Monday night in Phoenix. The night was dry and chill, the temperature hovering in the low 50s. A yellow-white slice of moon was rising above the mountains to the east. Lindsey and I fell against each other, walking out with arms entwined around backs and waists, her head nuzzled into my chest. A couple of cops looked on disapprovingly; we were still in uniform. A nurse coming on duty smiled. I felt a camera flash off to the side. God, I felt tired.

We stopped by a drive-through taqueria and picked up burritos. Then, back at home in the 1928 Monterey Revival house with the picture window on Cypress Street, Lindsey made martinis while I peeled off the bloody uniform. There was even blood on my boots. I took a long, hot shower, feeling the caked blood and dirt come off my skin.

"Are you as OK as you can be, History Shamus?"

She stood at the door as I toweled off. Then she handed me a drink, just the way I like it: Bombay Sapphire, dry, with one olive. She had changed into a gray sweatshirt and jeans, and her straight dark hair, parted in the middle, swept against her shoulder as she cocked her head. Her face, with its economical eyebrows, friendly lips, and fair skin, was never far from that look of ironic insolence that had first attracted me. When she wore her oval-shaped tortoise-shell glasses, as she was doing now, she looked impossibly sexy. But as we had cleaved together the past two years, I had learned more of the subtle tones of her expressions. Tonight, it conveyed safety, "we-ness," as she would say. She could soothe me with just her presence. I let the gin warm my throat before I tried to answer.

At ten minutes before midnight there was banging on the door. We were in bed, and I peeked out the front window to see half a dozen people clustered on the porch. Uniforms. Suits. One was Sharon Peralta. Beneath the porchlight was the unmistakably rigid carriage of Judge Peralta. I felt a chill creep up my feet.

"Oh my God," I said. "He must have…"

In a minute, they were arrayed around the living room. Kimbrough was there and made introductions: The woman in the pastel blue dress was Kathleen Markham, the chairwoman of the board of county supervisors. The fifty-something man in the blazer and polo shirt was the county manager, Dan Pickett. Sharon took my hand and looked at me through tears. A younger woman in a black pants suit, Lauren somebody, was with the county recorder. A couple of young deputies stood in the background. The judge, in a suit, moved naturally to the imposing leather chair that had been my grandfather's and eased himself down. Kimbrough looked like hell in the face, creased and ashen, but he had changed into a tailored navy suit and natty bow tie. I didn't want anyone to speak. I didn't want to know.

Finally, Kimbrough said, "We have a s i t u a t i o n."

"What?"

"How is he?" Lindsey said. "How is Peralta?"

"Oh, David," Sharon said, sighing. "He's the same. I realize what you must have thought. No, he's stable."

I sat cautiously on an ottoman. "What then?"

"David." It was Judge Peralta. His voice had its usual tone of deep but disengaged gravity. Did I just imagine the layer of exhaustion in it?

"We are here to ask you to be acting sheriff."

I heard Lindsey inhale sharply. I said, "Are you nuts?" I added, "Sorry, sir." I looked around. All of them were staring intently at me.

"We have a crisis, Mapstone," Kimbrough said. "Somebody who is still out there tried to kill the sheriff today. The sheriff may be out for a month. Or he may be..." He looked at Sharon and stopped.

"My point," he said, "is that the department is at a critical time. We don't know what brought on this attack. I have guards with the county supervisors. And we have to name an acting sheriff."

"What about the old sheriff?"

"He has declined," said Markham "He is already in Washington. He left right after the swearing in. And the timing just isn't right for him to stay on."

I was shaking my head. "What about the brass? Any one of them is qualified to be acting sheriff."

Kimbrough coughed and cleared his throat. "The senior bureau heads are all competing for the chief deputy job, Mapstone. It's politically delicate."

I just stared at him, not wanting to understand.

Kathleen Markham said. "The top officials in the sheriff's department are all ambitious men. Among the county supervisors, Bill Davidson has his supporters and Jack Abernathy has his. Even Mr. Kimbrough here has his backers." Kimbrough shifted uncomfortably. "We didn't have to be concerned with that when the obvious leader of the department was Peralta. Now, nobody wants to make a move that could be misinterpreted."

"That's not my problem."

"Mapstone," Markham said, "the brass all recommended you. It was the one thing they could agree on." My mind rewound the scene in Peralta's office with Jack Abernathy cursing me under his breath. That was the esteem the brass held me in. And I thought again, What did Peralta mean by the notation "Camelback Falls"?

Lindsey put a hand on my shoulder. I looked into the high ceiling of the living room, scanned the tall bookshelves and the ornate iron railing of the staircase, anything to avoid these faces.

"I am not qualified. And I don't even see how this is legal. The elected sheriff is alive. He is going to recover."

"At which point you will return power to him," said Markham. "But this is not only legal but necessary. Tonight we adopted a resolution." She waved her hand at the woman from the recorder's office, who passed me a legal-size page with thick black paragraphs and a seal cut into the paper. "It names you as acting sheriff of Maricopa County." She looked at Judge Peralta. "And we have a distinguished retired state appeals court judge to handle the swearing in."

I sat there listening, feeling an ache growing in my neck and back where Peralta had lurched into me and we had fallen to the floor. Pain and numbness and reality. I wanted to run from the room and lock myself away, just like I was ten years old.

"David," Kimbrough said. "You are the right person for this. You are a sheriff's academy graduate, the media know who you are, you're a smart guy, and you're disinterested. You're the one person everybody could agree on."

"Please stand, David." Judge Peralta lifted himself painfully out of Grandfather's chair. The effort shifted the knot on his red rep tie off to one side. "You know this is what my son would want."

Now he wasn't fighting fair.

The judge looked at Lindsey. "Do you have a Bible, Miss Adams?" She retrieved one from the tall bookshelves by the stairs, and he positioned her to hold it before me.

I felt my legs tense and then I was standing up, my right hand raised, my left on the rough black cover of Grandmother's family Bible. Lindsey gave me a secret smile. The burrito growled loudly in my stomach. In a raw voice, I repeated he oath from Judge Peralta.

Chapter Four

"Good morning, Sheriff."

Lindsey lay between my legs, kissing the inside of my thighs, brushing her soft hair across my awakening skin. Her hair color is just one notch lighter than black, but when the light hits it right you can make out some auburn, too. The light was hitting it right, the intense winter sun flooding joyfully through the tall bedroom window that faced Cypress Street.

"Acting sheriff," I whispered, my mouth feeling cottony and hung over.

"I've never blown the sheriff before."

"Lindsey!"

"Stop thinking, Dave." She nibbled, kissed, teased.

"But…"

After a long anticipatory ritual, she took me in her mouth.

She murmured something indecipherable. I moaned and clutched the sheets. Later I would think about my sleepless night, rewinding and playing yet again the events in the Immaculate Heart gym. Peralta festooned with tubes and wires, in a coma. The blood everywhere. Later I would think how, as Lindsey told me, I was lucky the first shot didn't come through Peralta and hit me. That worry pain in my middle, right below where my ribs met the breastbone, would resume, goaded by the memory of all the other times I had waited helplessly for word from a hospital. And I would stew about the events at midnight out in the living room, which suddenly had launched us all on a trajectory that seemed guaranteed to turn out badly. But that was later.

Lindsey murmured, and I moaned. She knew just how to play me. To hell with my dying friend, the sheriff. We had the deep history now, Lindsey and I. Three years ago I was lucky enough to stop by her cubicle to get help on a case. I had spent too many years entwined in love affairs with overcomplicated, overwrought women. Lindsey wasn't like all the others, as she said. She loved books. She loved sex. She had turned thirty the month before. But she was an old soul, my dark star, full of kindness and good sense and a brave heart. I had made love at twilight with Lindsey, and it didn't fill me with dread or sadness.

So I contracted the world to the two of us and stopped thinking. The sheets were getting comfortably old. The room smelled of sex. A wintering cardinal banged into the window, then fluttered away. My hands fluttered ecstatic against her fine dark hair.

Afterward, we held each other more tightly than usual, and we let go with reluctance when the phone reached the third ring.

"Good morning, Sheriff."

I cleared my throat and said, "I'm only the acting sheriff. Who are you?"

"Communications center, sir. I'm Sergeant Robin Greene," came the voice on the other end. I waited and she went on. "This is your morning briefing. Sheriff. I am the communications day watch commander."

I instinctively swung out of the bed. My feet felt swollen and creaky. I looked across the hall to the empty guest bedroom. Pasternak sat in the doorway watching me with his old gray tomcat eyes. Two years ago Peralta had lived in that room, during a time when he and Sharon were close to a rupture and life was getting way too complicated.

"We had a fairly busy night," Sergeant Greene went on. "We had an unauthorized prisoner release from the Durango Street Jail."

"What?"

"An inmate was released who shouldn't have been. He was down the railroad tracks before they even realized it. He's in for rape, a six-time loser."

"Good lord," I said.

"I know, sir. We've issued the standard statement to the media."

"We lose prisoners so often there's a standard statement'?"

"It's just procedure, sir. And there was a shooting overnight in District One, in Queen Creek. A six-year-old girl, she was supposed to testify in a murder trial today against a gang member."

"You're just a beam of sunshine, Sergeant Greene," I said. Lindsey looked at me quizzically and pulled the sheets over herself.

"Just the job, sir," Greene said. "No other county homicides last night. Phoenix had two, and Mesa had one, a drive-by. One chase involving DPS. Highway patrolman attempted to stop a vehicle at 2300 last night outside Buckeye. He initiated pursuit when the vehicle failed to stop. Other agencies joined in, and the suspect finally ran off the Stack as it headed into downtown Phoenix."

"Jesus," I said, imagining the tall freeway interchange near down-town where Interstates 10 and 17 came together. "How far down?"

"He fell seventy-five feet, and was unhurt. We have him in Madison Street Jail, sir."

"Don't let him go," I said.

"No, sir," she said. No humor in Sergeant Greene. "Shall we send your car and driver, Sheriff?"

"What?" Sheriff. The word suddenly sounded so strange. It came from old England. The "shire reeve," in old England a local government official, not really a law enforcement officer. The Sheriff of Nottingham. Rhode Island counties still called theirs "high sheriffs." Sergeant Robin Greene waited on the line.

"No," I said. "I'll take my own car."

◇◇◇

It was nearly 1:30 that afternoon before I could return to the haven of my office in the old courthouse. Past the retired highway patrolman who was the security guard in the lobby, up the four flights of circular stairway, my feet adding to the wear on the polished 1929 Spanish tile. Past the mostly empty floors, still richly appointed with dark woodwork and deco lighting fixtures. Somehow Phoenix had forgotten to tear down this wonderful old building. At the top of the stairway, I checked my watch again: 1:33. I would wait until two to check on Peralta.

Finally I turned my key, turned on the lights, and was alone in the high-ceilinged room with my books and old cases, just like my life used to be. A black-and-white portrait of Sheriff Carl Hayden, circa 1906, greeted me from the far wall. His hat-brim was straight, like his long, slender lips and his eyes fixed on some long-dead photographer. Phoenix's population was about 10,000 then. I gave Sheriff Hayden a little salute and stepped in, locking the door behind me. I needed some time alone.

"You did this job and you turned out OK," I said to the photo. "But I don't think I'll get to serve forty-two years in the Senate the way you did."

I hung up my dark blue suit coat and loosened the red Ferragamo tie Lindsey gave me for Christmas, sartorial armor for my first day as acting sheriff. Sinking into the ancient wooden desk chair, I propped up my feet and nursed the vente skim no-whip mocha I had carried over from Starbucks. Out the high windows I could hear the clatter and hum of downtown. I made myself breathe slower, deeper. It was an effort.

On the desk before me was the *Arizona Republic*, right where I left it that morning. Two-thirds of the front page was devoted to the Peralta shooting, including a sidebar on me, and the photo of Lindsey and me leaving the hospital wrapped around each other like eighth-graders. Only the expressions on our faces gave away the grimness of what we had come from. My face looked unfamiliar and tired. The story got things about half right, which was typical of the hometown press unless my friend Lorie Pope was doing the reporting. But none of the bylines were familiar. Maybe Lorie was on leave to write a book, an exposé of the bullshit of the Maricopa County Sheriff's Office.

I hated the cop bureaucracy that was represented by the crowded sheriff's administration building a block south. Only the smell of paper overcame the persistent odor of human beings in trouble and the human beings that dealt with them. Now I was in charge of the damned thing. The morning had gone by with a march of meetings, about next year's departmental budget, about the new HMO for department personnel, about the court-mandated sensitivity training classes for all deputies, about the lawsuit over last year's patrol car purchase. No wonder we just let prisoners walk away from the jail. We were in meetings all the time. I didn't say much. Nobody seemed to mind. The low expectations people had for me were obvious.

I spent an hour with the heads of the nine bureaus that made up the Sheriff's Office, and about all I could do was tell them I expected all to carry on with the same professionalism and commitment that Sheriff Peralta would demand. Go win one for the Gipper, who's still in critical condition. Kimbrough came in to update us on the investigation of the shooting. He had twenty-five detectives working on the case. Phoenix PD had offered another thirty cops if we wanted them. The FBI was pressing to be invited in. Nobody knew anything. The brass beat up Kimbrough pretty badly, especially Jack Abernathy, who was going rapidly from "indifferent" to "dislike" on my people meter. I made peace. They all looked at me with ambitious contempt.

I finished the mocha and hit the trash can with the first try. I thought maybe Lindsey and I could go to a Suns game tonight, just to unwind. I became nostalgic for my old life, which had existed until yesterday. The life where Lindsey and I were reading Rebecca West's *Black Lamb and Grey Falcon* to each other. Where I was going on my own through Niall Ferguson's *The Pity of War*, daydreaming that I could still write a controversial but wildly popular work of history just like that. Either way,

I was happy in my work in the old cases, where nobody cared except Peralta. I missed that life already.

Then I became aware of my heart, a metronome beating fast and heavy beneath my shirt. My heart pounded faster, insistently, self-consciously. In short order, it was making my hands tremble. My breathing came shorter, and that spot just south of the breastbone was pushing at me painfully. Maybe this was how a heart attack started.

When I heard the hand on the door, I jerked so hard I almost fell out of the chair.

I stood up hopefully. I could have used a long embrace from Lindsey right then, or even a repeat of the same old conversations with the security guard. But as I neared the door, the hand was still trying the lock. Now the jerking had some force behind it. The metal clacked back harshly. I could see a body, darkly dressed, leaning against the frosted glass of the door. But the old Jazz Age wood and hardware refused to give. Then the dark shape on the other side of the frosted glass faded.

I jerked the door open and the hallway before me was empty. I jogged down to the center of the building, where the stairs curved up, but there was no one. Down the other hallway was darkness, a little light reflecting off the glass of the old hanging lamps. Thirty feet down the hall all I could see was a green exit sign. Then a bright rectangle opened beneath the sign and a darkly dressed figure slipped through into the fire stairs.

Chapter Five

The city spreads across 1,400 square miles of the Salt River Valley. Fourteen hundred square miles of asphalt and manicured lawns. Fourteen hundred square miles of shopping malls, freeways, dusty barrios, and exclusive gated communities that tear into the sides of the surrounding mountains. At night, it becomes a breath-taking vision, billions of earth-born stars running out to the horizon. In the daytime, if the smog is light, the perpetual green of palm trees and golf courses and the craggy purple bare buttes give it an otherworldly look, especially to newcomers and Easterners. And that is nearly everybody. To me it is just home, all I knew until I was a teenager. Sometimes I think it is a great city, and I am filled with pride. Other times I am sickened by how much has been lost to the growth machine.

The city is an anti-city. It was built in opposition to the confined, shoulder-rubbing cities of the East, and in opposition to its bastard forebear, Los Angeles, in the West. It was built in opposition to reality—far from any crossroads, seaport, or reliable water source. Dams and canals and air-conditioning changed reality. So Phoenix grew up from a little farm town before World War II into a megalopolis of three million people.

As befits an anti-city. Phoenix's streets are wide and straight and predictable, running like a checkerboard atop the memories of alfalfa and cotton fields and citrus groves, and, before that, the irrigation canals of a vanished Indian nation. Today it's warehouses and ranch houses, poolside apartments and single-family detached houses with red tile roofs. It's single-story and spread out. A personal piece of the West for every family from Ohio and Indiana and New York. Up in the foothills and mountainsides, you find the faux adobe mansions that start at $3 million. But by that time, the streets get curvy and illogical.

The other exception in the street grid is Grand Avenue, which runs sideways through the checkerboard, straight out of downtown headed northwest. Before the interstate, it was the highway to L.A., four lanes of wanderlust set beside the tracks of the Santa Fe Railroad. On Tuesday afternoon, it was six lanes of bumper-to-bumper as commuters headed out to their subdivisions in Glendale, Peoria, and points beyond. I was the new acting sheriff but that got me exactly 30 miles an hour if I was lucky. I didn't care. I was in no hurry to get to a murder scene, but Kimbrough had demanded my presence. So much for going to the Suns game tonight. I turned up Sue Foley's "Young Girl Blues" on the CD and poked along.

An hour later, I turned off Grand, bumped across the Santa Fe tracks, and felt the gravel under my tires. Four brand-new sheriff's Ford Crown Victorias were arrayed off to the side of the road, along with one sun-bleached unit from the city of El Mirage. We were so far from the opulent resorts of Scottsdale we might as well have been on another planet. This looked more like the Third World.

It was a trailer park, if you dared use the latter word, sitting hard against the railroad tracks and hemmed in by the cinder block walls of a warehouse and a water pumping station. A dozen ancient house trailers sat on either side of a dirt-and-gravel cul-de-sac. Around them, as if blown there by innumerable dust storms, were rusting sheets of corrugated tin, unidentifiable hulks that maybe were automobiles once, refrigerator cartons stiffened by the sun, all manner of garbage. A little clot of brown-skinned children watched me warily as I parked.

I was still in my dark suit, and I was driving the BMW 325 convertible that my ex-wife left with me years before. So no wonder a uniformed deputy stopped me with some perturbed "sirs" and "excuse me's." He looked about eighteen. But Kimbrough stuck his head out the door to one trailer. "It's OK. This is Sheriff Mapstone."

I realized with a guilty jolt that I hadn't called to check on Peralta's condition this afternoon. I self-consciously hung my star over my jacket pocket and walked across broken beer bottles to the trailer.

Perhaps it had once been silver with festive blue stripes—trailers for sale or rent?—but had long ago become a bent box of rusting metal and some fading turquoise flashing. The smell hit me halfway to the door: sour, bitter, bent on conquest of all the senses. The smell of a body. I'd smelled worse. You don't work law enforcement four years in Arizona without getting a deep appreciation for what sun, heat, and confined spaces can do to human flesh. But it had been a long time.

"You OK?" Kimbrough asked, looking maddeningly poised and youthful. He was still wearing the gray tweed suit and highly polished cap-toe dress shoes from this morning's bureau heads' meeting. But the suit draped effortlessly on him. with no memory of the tough questions by the brass. He was not much younger than me, but still looked like one of those ads for the United Negro College Fund.

"I'm fine," I said, trying to growl it, feeling foolish. "What have you got?"

He motioned me to come in.

I tried breathing through my mouth. It did no good. I coughed and fought my gag reflex like hell. Three years ago I had been a college professor, with cares like getting published, fighting the post-structuralisms, and deflecting, gallantly, the come-ons of Heather Jameson in the twentieth century American history seminar that met Mondays, Wednesdays, and Fridays. Kimbrough said, "He's in the room to your right, Sheriff."

The floor seemed to give a little with an awful linoleum stickiness as I stepped inside. The little room was cramped with too much dirty old furniture, stacks of yellowing newspapers, big plastic bags full of empty aluminum cans and wine jugs. There wasn't enough space for the orange upholstered chair to overturn. So the chair sat at a cocky angle against a pile of newspapers, and a man was sprawled in it.

He had a large, black hole in his chest.

I looked back at Kimbrough.

"Remember him?"

I shook my head. Between rigor mortis, lividity, and impatient body gasses. the corpse didn't have what we would consider a face. But even the ghastly fun house mask that stared straight at me held no memories.

"That's Dean Nixon," Kimbrough said.

I stood straight and nearly beamed myself on the low ceiling. Something was coming down the railroad track straight for me, and I didn't have time to move.

"You were a deputy with him, right?" Kimbrough said.

I nodded. "Jesus. I haven't seen him in twenty years."

I stepped back out of the trailer, feeling the stickiness clinging to my shoes. Kimbrough followed me. It was only about 5:30, but the daylight was nearly gone. The sky above the White Tank Mountains was washed with brilliant orange and rust. A single cloud to the north stood out like a pink-and-white cotton ball. If you painted the Arizona sky realistically nobody would believe it. We walked far enough away that the only smell was the familiar mixture of Phoenix smog and dust.

Dean Nixon. He was a forgotten figure in my personal history. I had joined the Sheriff's Office halfway through college, full of idealism and restlessness. Despite a lifelong attraction to books and ideas, I had wanted to be a doer, not some pasty egghead in an ivory tower. I think I had a vague plan of going on to get a law degree. But I also had a high school buddy who had become a deputy sheriff. He told me I'd be great at the job. His name was Dean Nixon.

Somehow the department took me. I spent four years on the job, mostly as a patrol deputy. The jail held no fascination for me, and the administrative bullshit increasingly bored me.

On the side, concealed from most of my colleagues, I finished my degree in history and went on to get a master's. Then the Ph.D., and a chance to teach at a well-respected college in the Midwest. The world of ideas had me by the mind and the heart. I left law enforcement behind as a cherished youthful adventure. And although I stayed in touch with Peralta for the next twenty years, the connection with Dean Nixon had begun to lade even before I left the department.

Imagine having the name Nixon in the mid-1970s. In fact, Dean was handsome and magnetic in a rough way, with dry, wheat-blond hair and a tall frame that muscled out in high school working summers on Texas oil rigs. Women would walk up to him and give him their phone numbers. I saw it happen more than once. He had the inevitable nickname "Dick Nixon," but that held more irony than most people realized.

"When did you last hear from him?" Kimbrough said.

"Who knows?" I said. "Maybe 1980."

I realized with a pang of guilt that I hadn't even thought to look for him at my high school reunion last fall. I never imagined I'd find him like this. Law enforcement is full of unhappy career endings. Retired cops who put the service revolver in their mouths. Dean never seemed like that. He played the guitar and laughed a lot. Last I heard he was dating a doctor. I imagined he'd retired to the happy life of a kept man.

"He's been gone from the department for years," Kimbrough said. "He made ends meet as a bounty hunter and security guard."

I looked around us. "Not much making ends meet."

"No," Kimbrough said. He licked his lips and adjusted his suit coat. "The guy had a service record with lots of brutality complaints. A tough guy. Didn't get along with his bosses, either. Went through three marriages. Counseling for alcohol abuse. Looked like the wine department of Circle K in his refrigerator."

I said, "He was just a kid I knew in high school."

Kimbrough said, "You believe in destiny, Sheriff?"

I kicked at the ground and ruined my loafers in the dust. I realized the frustration and anger that had been building in me. Yeah, and insecurity But it was too late. "What a joke. Sheriff." I said. "I'm just the chump you guys decided on while Peralta's down."

The glass crunched under our feet, opaque shards of beer bottles mashed into the timeless topsoil of the desert. "Is that what you think?"

"You tell me. Captain Kimbrough."

He smiled unhappily. "Maybe that's what some of them think. I don't know. I think you're a good cop, Mapstone. Maybe because you and I are the only people in Arizona law enforcement with good taste in clothes."

He made me laugh. It was true. "So what is it?"

He shook his head. "They need a sheriff. The brass agreed on it. It's the first time Abernathy and Davidson have agreed on anything in the fifteen years I've been in this department."

He faced me. We had walked as far as we could, and stood above a bleak ditch filled with garbage and standing water.

"Just go with it, David," he said. "Hell, fuck with 'em if you want. You're the sheriff. The real deal. For now at least. Look at it this way: if Peralta recovers, you're looking out for his interest." He paused and all we heard was the deep growl of the trucks out on Grand Avenue. "If things don't work out, well, you and I will both be looking for new jobs."

"I had to drive a long damned way for a pep talk." I said. It came out badly. "I mean, thanks. Consider yourself acting chief of detectives."

"But…"

"Nope," I said. "I'm the sheriff. You have the job. What did you say about fucking with them? Now go find Peralta's shooter." I walked toward the BMW, feeling bad for Dean Nixon and sick of this day. "I'm going to check on him, then have a martini with my girlfriend and go see some hoops."

"Damn it, Mapstone," Kimbrough said. "That's what this is about. We've found the damned trail of Peralta's shooter, right here."

I stopped in my tracks, then faced him.

"What the hell?"

He reached into his coat pocket and pulled out a clear plastic evidence envelope. It held a business card. I took the bag and peered through the plastic. It was an MCSO card. "Mike Peralta, Sheriff," it said.

"What the hell?" I mumbled, then turned it over. In block handwritten letters was a name. "Leo O'Keefe," and a phone number in the city.

I handed the bag back, feeling a numbness in my hand, as if I'd touched something toxic.

"That was found in the pocket of our deceased former brother officer back there," Kimbrough said. "You know what it's talking about?"

I pulled off my coat and draped it over my arm. It was almost dark but it suddenly felt hot.

"Leo O'Keefe," I said, "was involved in a shoot-out in Guadalupe. Years ago. May 31, 1979. Two deputies were murdered. Two suspects were killed. Leo was arrested as an accomplice. So was his girlfriend." I licked the dust off my lips. My stomach hurt again. "Two of the deputies on that call were Nixon and Peralta."

Kimbrough was impressed. "You're a hell of a departmental historian, Sheriff."

I said, "I was there."

Out on the highway, a truck downshifted loudly and knocked away some of the images going through my mind.

"I was there."

Chapter Six

Peralta and I could work an entire shift and never say five words. That was just the way he was. It drove rookies crazy. They were already intimidated by his size and stage presence, that way he seemed to fill up a room just by walking in. And when he didn't say anything, they might spend an entire shift trying to get a conversation started. Not me. Three years before, when I ran my first training shift, I realized he was most comfortable sitting in the heart of a long silence. It was also good for police work: listening and watching, while others revealed themselves. It was my first eureka moment with him.

That seemed a long time ago. He was a sergeant now, but we rode together this night as part of a county plan to double up deputies and save gasoline. Last month, it had been a ban on driving more than fifty miles during a shift. Energy crisis. Inflation. It was always something. Riding with the sergeant kept me off the most routine calls. But it didn't matter this shift. We were bored as hell.

So much of police work is bone-achingly dull. Especially a shift like we were having, where even a minor accident or a low-grade burglary report would have been a welcome break. Instead, we cruised slowly through the unincorporated roads that ran off the dry riverbed, several miles of cinder block buildings, high cyclone fences strung with concertina wire, and some of the nastiest bars and massage parlors in the Valley. Neither Tempe nor Scottsdale wanted the land. So it stayed under county jurisdiction. But today even Ace's Tavern and Terry's Swedish Massage Institute ("real coeds") were quiet.

Peralta drove. He had new mirrored sunglasses that totally obscured his eyes. It unnerved people who looked at him, and I knew that secretly pleased him. From the passenger seat, I watched the streets without appearing to watch. That, I had learned early on the job, was part of the demeanor of a veteran. To rubberneck or glance to-and-fro marked you as a rookie, or, worse, a hotdog. And I listened to the radio without appearing to listen. That yielded little. A burglary report out by Williams Air Force Base. An auto accident west of Phoenix.

Peralta finally said, "Mapstone..." But he never finished the sentence.

"Nine-nine-nine! Nine-nine-nine!" A shout burst out of the radio speaker.

First I thought it was garble. Did we really hear that? Then, all nerve endings and stomach acid.

"Fuck," Peralta said, turning up the speaker. The code for officer needs emergency assistance was "999." It was the doomsday call for any street cop.

"Unit identify yourself and your 10-20," came back a cool female voice. The dispatcher wanted his location. But all we heard was the empty air. Sweat congealed under my uniform shirt.

I didn't recognize the voice, but we probably had two dozen patrol units scattered around the east county, not including the lake patrol. The inside of the car suddenly seemed unbearably hot. Peralta impatiently fiddled with the radio's squelch control, but we still heard nothing.

"Who the hell was that?" he demanded, to no one in particular.

The voice was so distorted by panic and static it could have been anybody. I said, "Nixon has some rookie with him." A rookie would commit that kind of unforgivable breach of radio protocol: failing to identify your unit first.

Peralta grunted and picked up the microphone. But the department had a procedure for everything, and the dispatcher was already ahead of him. She ordered all east-side units to switch to channel two and give their locations, to see who was missing. Dean Nixon called *in safely from Chandler. I had slandered a rookie without cause, not for the last time. I gave our "10-20" but it was changing rapidly.*

Peralta wheeled the big Chrysler south and gunned the V-8 police high-performance special. We shot out of the riverbed and flew at 80mph through Tempe. Hayden Road turned into McClintock. The sun slipped behind Hayden Butte and we were in half twilight.

"What?" I said.

Peralta compressed his lips violently, taking away half the real estate between his nose and his chin.

"It's Matson and Bullock," he said. "I bet you."

"Reserves?"

"Matson's a reserve deputy but Bullock is full-time. Usually works the day shift at the jail."

In Peralta's shorthand, that meant he was an old-timer, close to retirement.

He sensed what I was thinking, an eerie quality he had. He said, "We were shorthanded this shift. But I stuck 'em down in Guadalupe. Nothing ever happens there on a weeknight but a family fight."

"You sure about that?" I cracked, partly to ease my tension. Peralta retreated behind his mirrored shades. He got on channel one and tried to raise them. No response came back but a testy dispatcher telling him to keep the channel clear for emergency traffic.

We hit Baseline Road and turned west, into the radiant pink sunset. We swept through south Tempe, where new subdivisions were chewing up the old farmland at an alarming rate.

Five minutes after a "999" call we still didn't know who was involved or where they were. I said aloud, "How fucked up is this?"

But Peralta seemed to know. He switched frequencies and broadcast his theory. Indeed, Matson and Bullock, in unit 4-L-20, had not checked in. Peralta demanded to know their last location.

"56th Street and Guadalupe Road," the dispatcher said, obviously reading from a log. "Stated they were at the convenience store."

"Send all responding units to that location," Peralta ordered. He re-holstered the microphone and switched on the toggles for the emergency lights. The speedometer needle passed 90.

"Why don't we wait for the cavalry," I said, realizing how close to Guadalupe we were.

Peralta said, *"Too many cops will just get in the way."*

I nervously fingered the Speedloaders on my belt. Peralta had been in a dozen firefights, and he'd been in Vietnam. In three years on the job, I'd never done more than draw down on an occasional burglar.

The radio was alive now. The dispatcher repeated the address. But I knew exactly where it was. Guadalupe was a little closet of a town notched between Phoenix and Tempe, walled off by Interstate 10. It had been settled by Yaqui Indians displaced by the Mexican Revolution in the early 1900s, and it still looked like a poor Mexican village. Right across the line from Tempe's burgeoning suburban neighborhoods was this little huddle of whitewashed adobe buildings and dirt streets. And right now it was about to get scary.

The furrows of a cotton field swept past off the side of the road. The South Mountains loomed ahead. *"It's probably a fake call,"* Peralta said. But his brow was creased. He didn't believe it. He had the cop's sixth sense, better than any of us.

We turned onto 56th Street off Baseline and rolled in the last half mile with no lights, not even headlights. The sense of speed, darkness, and the bulk of the cruiser made everything seem like it was past tense. I saw people run inside small houses.

In the distance, the orange ball of the Union 76 gas sign glowed reassuringly. We bumped into a gravel parking lot, empty except for a sun-bleached Pinto that probably belonged to the clerk.

"Fuck," Peralta said. *"Put us rolling 10-6."* I told the dispatcher we were on the scene. No other sheriff's car was in sight.

"Go in and ask the clerk," he said, and I opened the door. But his hand suddenly caught my arm.

I turned back in the car and my eyes followed his gaze.

We both spoke in unison: *"Holy shit."*

Five minutes later in the twilight and we wouldn't have seen it. It was an alley, maybe 500 feet to the south, past a cinder block wall, an abandoned adobe house, and some mangled old cottonwood trees. I could clearly see the rear bumper and trunk of a sheriff's patrol car. Two pairs of boots lay in the dirt, the soles facing toward us. They were attached to bodies wearing uniforms, splayed out on their backs on either side of the car. Then I saw movement and two men were over one of the bodies. They were going through his pockets.

I unsnapped my holster and drew my service revolver. Peralta floored the Chrysler and we shot across the street, into the gravel alley, past the adobe house and the cinder block wall. A scene quickly materialized: a patrol car parked directly behind a ratty blue Chevy, two deputies faceup on the dirt, two other men standing over them and carrying automatic weapons.

Peralta slammed the gearshift into park. I pulled up my door handle. The windshield disappeared. Sharp glass fragments sprayed my face like chunks of hard, hot ice. My ears rang from the noise of the shots. Then there was nothing between me and a bulky, sunburned man with long yellow hair and filthy jeans. He was cradling an M-16.

I sighted him down the barrel of my service revolver, raising it as fast as I could. My hand shook violently. Sweat ran off my wrist. I was still stuck in the car, now absurdly exposed. He aimed at me, tensed, and I knew I had lost the race.

Then the air exploded and his middle turned into a dark red mess. He jolted back in the air as if slapped by a giant hand, then collapsed on the ground. Peralta walked toward him, a big man in a tan uniform, still holding out the shotgun for lethal business. I rolled out onto the dirt, keeping my head down.

Under the car, I saw jeans and black biker boots run toward us from the front of the other cruiser. An angry screaming, a sharp string of gunfire. Then another low boom from the direction of Peralta.

I forced myself off the ground, and we were alone. Peralta and me and four dead men. A layer of gunsmoke lingered as a chest-level cloud, ghostly in the fading light. It almost seemed tinged red with blood turned aerosol by the buckshot.

For the longest time the night grew around us and was utterly silent. Then I heard calls for help in Spanish, and finally the sounds of sirens, growing louder.

That's how I remembered it.

Chapter Seven

Lindsey wrinkled her nose as if something smelled bad. "The seventies," she said. "Yuck."

"I thought you liked the music," I challenged. A light band of freckles spread across her nose. You'd miss it in most lights. Her tiny gold nose stud gleamed in her left nostril. She was out of uniform, wearing black jeans and an oversized gray sweater.

"I like the music, sometimes, because it's campy and fun. I also like Sleater-Kinney and Beethoven, Dave. I'm unpredictable."

"I love that."

She studied her shot glass, bent down close to the table, and sipped off the golden meniscus of Glenlivit, her winter drink. "But the seventies seems pretty gross." She arched her eyebrow. "You baby boomers."

"Sex, drugs, and rock 'n' roll, baby."

She brushed back a strand of dark hair that had fallen over her right eye. "I bet you had a pair of polyester pants."

"I'll deny it. But I also had a pair of platform shoes. Made me six-foot-eight."

"It's all coming back in style." She curled her lips slyly.

"OK, I agree. Yuck."

We sat at a back table in the My Florist Cafe, a neighborhood bar that had taken over a former flower shop on McDowell. The Willo Historic District started to the north, where a neighborhood of 1920s houses somehow had survived Phoenix's destructive ways. Below McDowell Road, lovely old neighborhoods had been obliterated by an underground freeway in the 1980s and for years it looked like the victim of a small-scale nuclear war. Now the area was slowly coming back. New upscale apartments and condos were going up next to Margaret Hance Park. The bungalows in the palm-lined streets around Kenilworth School were being rehabbed. Even the stark coppery box of the city library—everybody called it "The Toaster"—was looking more appealing.

I was just grateful for a place to relax close to home. I was working on my second martini, feeling light and calm for the first time all day, retelling the twenty-one-year-old story of the Guadalupe shootout. It was the easy unwinding when we told each other of our day. We never made it to the Suns game.

Lindsey said, "And you were how old when this happened?"

"Twenty-three."

"Twenty-three." She looked me over. "I bet you were hot stuff, History Shamus."

"Nobody thought so," I said.

"I doubt that, Dave. But if the shootout ended with the dirtballs getting killed, how does that tie into the shootings of Peralta and Nixon?"

I said, "It wasn't over yet."

I again walked her back twenty years and through what happened next. With the second suspect down, I pulled myself off the gravel and checked the two deputies on the ground for pulses. They were both faceup dead. Then I looked toward this old blue Chevy, still idling directly ahead of the sheriff's cruiser, and a head bobbed above the seat and disappeared. I drew down and ordered them out. Peralta came up on the other side of the car and chambered a new round in the shotgun. Then Nixon and his partner rolled in. A woman's voice begged us not to kill them.

They slowly crawled out of the backseat. The woman looked like the girl next door, if you stuck the girl next door right in the middle of a multiple homicide: surfer-girl blond hair, straight and parted in the middle, prom-queen face. Her companion was a small man with very long black hair. They were younger than me. She started crying and talking. I told her to shut up, Mirandized her, and pushed her down into the gravel and burrs. I cuffed her to await a search from a female deputy. Then the guy. Peralta had him on his knees, the shotgun not six inches from his face. I cuffed him and pushed him face-down next to her, ordered him to shut up, too.

"You guys didn't just beat confessions out of suspects back then?" Lindsey smiled darkly.

"We were very professional," I said. "I didn't want them to get shot in all the confusion and adrenaline. Cops get nervous trigger fingers when two of their colleagues have just been shot down like dogs."

Lindsey finished her scotch. "These two in the backseat. They were involved?"

I nodded. "The guy was named Leo O'Keefe. He went to prison as an accessory. The girl, Marybeth Watson, was his girlfriend. She got probation, I think. They were all Okies, in the big city."

Lindsey stared at the table, her long, slender fingers making a V around the shot glass. "And Leo O'Keefe was the name written on the back of Peralta's business card, found in Dean Nixon's pocket..."

"Right," I said. "It's weird. It's a new card. Peralta is listed as sheriff, not chief deputy."

"Would he have been in contact with Nixon?" she asked.

"I can't imagine it," I said. "He never said anything to me."

"So where does Leo O'Keefe come in?"

Two more drinks appeared.

"On the house, for the new sheriff," the waitress said. She looked like one of the models who sang behind Robert Palmer on the video for "Addicted to Love." I recalled her name was Jodie.

"Acting sheriff," I said. "And you know I have to pay. But thanks." I suddenly felt deflated and exhausted. At the bar, people were talking like they had a future. Good-looking young people with leather jackets and cell phones. Peralta lay a few blocks away near death. I turned back to Lindsey. "Kimbrough checked on O'Keefe, and he escaped from prison two weeks ago. It's not inconceivable that he's out to get revenge on the officers involved in his arrest. The phone number went to a fleabag hotel out on Van Buren, but a man matching O'Keefe's description left two days ago."

Her blue eyes flashed alarm. "Dave, if he went after Nixon and Peralta…" She stared at me. "You were at Guadalupe, too."

I started on the third martini, wishing I hadn't, feeling the chill gin warm my throat. "Every law enforcement agency in the West is looking for this guy."

"Jesus!" Lindsey leaned toward me, elbows on the table. Her sleek forearms peeked out of the sweater sleeves. "Are you packing?"

I pulled back my coat to reveal the Python in a black nylon holster on my belt.

"You and that damned revolver," she said.

I patted it lightly. "It'll never jam."

She wrinkled her nose again. Like all the younger cops, she preferred a semiautomatic pistol. It was fast and held more ammunition. She unconsciously put her right hand on her backpack, which held her Glock.

"I can't believe you," she whispered. Her eyes did a subtle once-around-the-room. The crowd at the bar laughed uproariously at something.

We walked the half mile home, alongside streets with sparse weeknight traffic. Up Fifth Avenue to Cypress, past the big old palms and the stucco houses. The air was dry and cold. It might get down to the low 40s tonight. Lindsey had a tension in her stride, and I knew she was quietly aggravated that I had decided we should walk to the hospital, stop at My Florist, and walk home when some nut was out there who might be after me, too. I looked behind us, but the street was empty except for the shadows of the palm trees. The buzz of a helicopter—police or TV news—came from the direction of downtown.

I decided against telling her about my mysterious visitor that afternoon. After I saw the fire door open, I went back in my office and called the security desk downstairs. But the guard said he never saw anyone come out. Leo O'Keefe? It was probably just somebody who was lost and looking for the marriage license bureau in the courthouse basement. Cops could get so paranoid. So could history professors.

Finally she asked, "What about Nixon's partner, the rookie? Is he safe."

"He's dead," I said. She looked at me wide-eyed. "No, not that way. Cancer. He died in 1995."

Time to change the subject. "Lindsey," I said. "Have you ever heard of Camelback Falls?"

"Sounds like a new resort on Camelback Mountain. Just add water," she said. "What is it, really?"

"I don't know. It was a notation in Peralta's datebook, next to my name. I saw it yesterday when I went for his insulin. But I've never heard of anything like that."

She said, "David Mapstone, native Phoenician and Arizona history expert stumped? Let me write down the date."

"I also had a run-in with Jack Abernathy, who came in Peralta's office while I was there. He was acting strange."

"He is strange, Dave. The deputies call him the Planet Abernathy, because he's so far out in orbit."

We crossed Monte Vista, one block to Cypress. She went on, "Anyway, I don't know what Camelback Falls is. Maybe it's like Niagara Falls."

She stopped and gave me a kiss, all tongue and passion. She giggled, a very un-Lindsey-like action. "I'm yours 'til Camelback Falls, Dave."

Then she took my hand snugly in hers, and we resumed our fast walk home.

Chapter Eight

By 10 a.m. Wednesday, I had already spent two hours in the records bureau, looking through case records of the Guadalupe shootout. I'm not a morning person, but I wasn't sleeping. Until two days before, I could come here as a nobody. Or a curiosity: that former history professor who worked for Peralta. Now I created a sensation. Records clerks scurried forward to meet me, to find every file I sought, to cover their asses. With difficulty, I persuaded them to return to work and let me have some quiet. Hell, I was still nobody, and would happily return to that state as soon as Peralta popped his eyes open and started making his usual demands.

But two days after the shooting, that still hadn't happened. The night before, we sat with Sharon as nurses came and went from his bedside like initiates in an obscure cult. We watched his heartbeat on the scratchy electronic line of the EKG, watched his chest rise and fall to the command of the respirator. I had asthma as a child, and the fear of suffocating still lingers. The respirator scares the hell out of me. The swelling of his brain had gone down, the doctors told Sharon. And their devices measured brain activity, a good sign. But he was still out cold. Sharon sat by his bed speaking to him in her soothing coloratura, a voice even nicer in person than on the radio. But the only response was the steady trace of a heartbeat, a blue-white line on the screen by his bed.

With that memory, I finished off the remains of a bagel, took another sip of my mocha, and went back to the work before me. The trauma of that May evening so many years before was reduced to four file folders on a table. Paper records. The department was moving backward, putting files into the computer database that could be viewed by deputies using laptops in the field. But that effort petered out with documents dated around 1990. I was looking at antiques of law enforcement record-keeping.

The files were a mess of incident reports, witness statements, news clippings, detectives' notes, and court transcripts. Some faxed pages were almost entirely faded out. But sheet by sheet, the events revealed themselves. There was even a copy of the arrest report of Leo Martin O'Keefe and Marybeth Watson, with my signature and badge number—"D.P. Mapstone, 5718"—at the bottom of the page. I didn't remember being there for the booking, but obviously I was. It was a long time ago.

The memory of the files was incomplete, but it went like this: At approximately 6:45 P.M. on the evening of May 31, 1979, sheriff's deputies Harold Matson and Virgil Bullock stopped a suspicious vehicle in an alley in Guadalupe. The occupants of the car apparently opened fire on the deputies as they approached. Matson and Bullock never knew what hit them. Their .38 Special service revolvers weren't even drawn.

At 7:02 P.M., Sergeant Mike Peralta and Deputy David Mapstone arrived on the scene. They encountered the suspects, who immediately opened fire on them with automatic weapons. Peralta killed two suspects. (Mapstone was pretty fucking worthless, though the record happily omitted that fact). The two dead suspects were Billy McGovern and Troyce Meadows. They were prison escapees from Oklahoma, in for armed robbery and, at ages twenty-three and twenty-four, carrying hardcore records. They had escaped from the state prison in McAlester the previous July by hiding in a laundry truck.

Charged as accessories were Leo and Marybeth. They were Okies, too. Just kids: Leo was twenty-one and Marybeth was seventeen. Billy McGovern was Leo's cousin. Somehow the four had hooked up on the afternoon of May 31. Then the paper trail faded and disappeared. The files held no statements from Leo or Marybeth. It was the frustration of dealing with records that had been picked over a period of years, then relocated as the department grew, and finally neglected until the past reached out and threatened us. I made a note to call over to the County Attorney's Office. Maybe they had a more complete file.

Still, the outcome was clear from court papers and press clippings. Leo and Marybeth were charged as accessories. Arraigned as a juvenile, Marybeth received five years' probation. Leo agreed to a plea-bargain, accessory to assault on a police officer, and got a year in the state prison. It jarred me to see the name of his public defender, Hector Gutierrez, who was now one of the best known white-shoe lawyers in town. Back then, he had been called "Red Hector" for his radical politics and courtroom diatribes against "the system."

A frayed clipping: Leo O'Keefe, imprisoned for his role in a 1979 killing of two deputies, was charged with the murder of another inmate. Then it was life for Leo, which in Arizona meant more than seven years and out on good behavior. So he was capable of killing.

A mug shot from 1979: Leo looking scared and a little stoned. A stupid kid with stringy black hair over his shoulders and black plastic-framed glasses. But he had an old-man's face, with a knobby chin and raw cheekbones. He hardly looked the role of the hardened killer.

Then I saw myself. My God, I looked young, so damned young. My photo stared out from an article on the shooting. Peralta was there, too. I had forgotten he was sporting a thick bandito mustache back then. And even though in my mind's eye Peralta was always the same, he, too, looked impossibly youthful. The article was by Lorie Pope of the *Arizona Republic*. She was a twenty-one-year-old cub reporter then. I wondered what she remembered about the case.

"So how's it hanging, Sheriff?"

It was Bill Davidson, his long, handsome face peering around a set of filing cabinets.

"Oh, somehow I'm still employed," I said. "How are you?" It was strange to see these senior commanders, who had mostly regarded with me indifference, suddenly chatting like old friends. Davidson was OK compared to his peers. He'd never treated me like I had two heads and open sores.

"Oh, getting too old to do this stuff." He sighed and edged against the filing cabinet, a lean uniformed man with careless posture. "Every day I come to work thinking I've seen just how cruel human beings can be to each other, and every night I go home with a new lesson I didn't want to know." His face regarded me with easy brown eyes, a thick gray mustache, long age lines in the right places on skin that was sundried and taut. It was an adult man's face, authentic but out of place in an age of teenage boy beauty.

I couldn't help but notice the long whitish scar on the side of his neck. It came up out of his collar and stopped just below his left ear. Davidson got that when I was still a rookie. He was the first on the scene of a guy trying to kill his baby daughter with a machete. Davidson pulled the kid out of the way and took the brunt of the blade in the side of his neck and shoulder. It was one of the bravest things I ever heard of when I was on the streets.

"I see you're in uniform," he said.

"I brief the media at noon," I said. "It seemed like the right thing."

He drew his mustache down distastefully. "I don't envy you that," he said. "Little light reading?" He nodded toward the array of files on the table before me.

I told him what I was doing. He said, "Sheriff, you pay detectives to do this kind of thing for you. You don't have to do this."

"Oh, I just wanted to see." Truth was, I desperately needed something to occupy my time besides going to meetings and worrying about Peralta.

Davidson shook his head. "Poor old Matson and Bullock," he said. "Talk about the wrong place at the wrong time. I remember right where I was that day: flat on my back with strep throat. Got it from my kid." I didn't know Davidson personally back then, and he probably didn't know of my involvement in the shooting.

He said, "That killing shook up this department for years. It hit home. Hell, Harry Matson had been my training officer when I was a rookie. After that, we knew Phoenix wasn't the same place any more." The long etchings in his face tensed and deepened. "People were just crazy, vicious for no reason. They called us 'pig.' They'd set up ambushes for us. Pull out guns when all that happened is they were stopped for some petty-ass traffic violation."

"What do you know about this O'Keefe?"

"Not a damned thing," Davidson said.

"I just wonder if he's capable of coming back to get revenge."

Davidson said, "It's always the ones you don't think about. Not the guys that stand up in court and threaten to kill your family. Prison has a way of dealing with most big talkers. No, it's guys like this little prick."

We both noticed Lindsey standing behind him. Davidson turned suddenly crimson. "Pardon my language," he said, and excused himself. Davidson was at least ten years older than me, in a generation of male cops that had been forced to accept women colleagues. But some still held these quaint taboos and social customs from an earlier time. In the right setting, it was kind of endearing.

Lindsey cocked an eyebrow. "We should all avoid little pricks, Sheriff."

"You are so bad." I looked at her straight on. She was in civilian clothes, a white, oxford-y blouse, short black skirt, sheer black stockings, black shoes with thick heels. She loved her monochromes, and with her hair and coloring it worked to stunning effect. I said what I thought: "Will you marry me? My God, you are beautiful."

She smiled. "I'm glad you think so." She reached down and scratched my shoulder. "You're pretty sexy in uniform, Dave. This is a part of you I've rarely seen."

I told her about the press briefing.

She leaned down and whispered in my ear, "Sometime you'll have to wear your uniform at home, give me the discipline I need, Sheriff." Her soft hair ran across my neck and face. I was instantly hard. Right there in Central Records.

"You're blushing, Dave," she said. "I thought all you guys who came of age in the seventies had no inhibitions."

"I'm not blushing." I said, feeling the heat running out into my face.

"Who's that?" She put a long finger on the mugshot of Leo O'Keefe.

"He doesn't look like a cop killer," she said after I told her. "Just looks like a kid." She pulled up a chair next to me and sat, crossing her fine dark-stockinged legs. "Now these guys." She reached over to the prison photos of McGovern and Meadows. "You can see the sociopath in their eyes. But this kid, what was he doing out with the other two?"

"He was this one's cousin," I tapped McGovern's surly face. "He and his girlfriend Marybeth somehow hooked up with them."

Lindsey bit her lower lip. "What a mess. Could those kids have even done anything to stop the shooting?"

"I don't know," I said. "I was trying to find their statements to refresh my memory. But a lot of the deputies thought they got off too easy, probation for her and a year for O'Keefe. But he's a loser. Iced a guy in prison and they tacked life onto his sentence."

She rubbed her hand over my back. "Oh, Dave, you're not that hard. You know how bad luck comes to people."

I nodded, felt a pang of something like compassion, and put my hand on her thigh. Right there in Central Records.

Lindsey said, "But if he tries to hurt you, I'll put a nice tight pattern of hollow-point ammunition in his chest, reload, shoot him again, and then read him his rights.

"I'm actually here on a mission, Dave." she went on, absently picking through the files. "You asked about Camelback Falls."

"Yes." I lowered my voice. "It was the notation in Peralta's calendar."

"Camelback Falls was the name of a house," she said. "It's still there, actually. On the south face of the mountain. Anyway, does the name Jonathan Ledger mean anything to you?"

"The sex guy?" I asked.

"You are the sex guy," she whispered as I stroked her leg. "Dave, let me concentrate. Yes, Ledger wrote *The Sex Instructions* and *More Sex Instructions.* Best-sellers, as you know. Not that I've ever read them. He owned the house until his death in 1989. He called it Camelback Falls. Maybe it was some wordplay on Falling Water."

"Who owns the house now?" I asked.

"Some rich guy who lives in North Carolina. The house has changed hands five times since Ledger died. The current owner is trying to get a permit to demolish it and build something grander. But the house hasn't been called Camelback Falls since Ledger. When I called the Realtor today she didn't even know that was what it was called."

I sat back in the chair. Now I was more baffled than ever. What could Peralta have wanted to know from me about Jonathan Ledger's house on Camelback Mountain?

"Thanks, beautiful," I said. "You're pretty smart for a propeller head."

She licked her lips, "What are you doing for lunch, Sheriff?"

"Media briefing," I said sadly. "But afterward..."

"Actually," she said, "I have another mission. I'm going to the briefing, too. That's why I'm kind of preppy-looking today, and I know that look really turns you on, Dave. But I am your new bodyguard."

"I work alone, ma'am," I said, deepening my voice. "Anyway, the cyber-terrorists of the world won't take a holiday while you baby-sit me."

"Sorry, Dave. You have to be accompanied by a deputy from now on. It's new policy. So you can have me, or some knuckle-dragger from the patrol bureau. Kimbrough is getting very ticked off that you're just wandering around unprotected. And so am I." She sat back, luminous, smiling, proud of herself.

I smiled, too, and said, "Well, don't expect me to get any work done."

Chapter Nine

The phone's ring broke me out of a nightmare about Peralta, shadows at my office door, and suffocating on the end of a respirator hose. But when I picked it up there was only silence on the line, silence in the dark bedroom, Lindsey's hand against the sweat cooling on my back.

Then a voice said, "David Mapstone?"

"That's me."

"Acting Sheriff David Mapstone?"

If this was a telemarketer, I was going to get homicidal. Instead, the voice, a man's voice—average, unremarkable, baritone—said, "This is Leo O'Keefe."

I sat up straight, turned on the light and mouthed the words "Leo O'Keefe" to Lindsey. She angled out of bed and disappeared down the hall.

"Leo, we need to talk to you."

"I saw the news," he said. "You're after me."

"You're an escaped convict," I said. The little pinpoint of pain pushed at my middle. "You know the detectives suspect you shot Sheriff Peralta."

"I didn't," the voice said calmly. "Who are you, David Mapstone? Why are you the acting sheriff?"

Beats the hell out of me, I thought. Lindsey came back in the room, a cell phone at her ear. She pantomimed with the other hand: Keep him talking.

"I'm nobody, Leo. I'm the department historian. I was the one they got to fill in after the sheriff was wounded."

"I'm sorry he's hurt," the voice said. He didn't remember me from Guadalupe, or my name, anyway.

"What about Dean Nixon," I said. "Did you try to contact him?"

The line went silent. Finally, "That's right. Have you talked to Deputy Nixon about me?"

"Leo, you've got to turn yourself in. I give you my word, you will be treated well."

He laughed. "Yeah," he said. "I know about that." His voice picked up momentum, edged up half an octave. "Mapstone, they can't let any of this come out. That's why Peralta was shot."

I started to speak, but he cut me off.

"I have information for you," he said, now speaking frantically. "I can't explain now. If you're interested, walk to the pay phone at the Jack in the Box at Third Avenue and McDowell. I can see if you come alone or not, and I can see if cops are in the parking lot. Make sure you walk."

"Leo…"

"Come now, Mapstone. Your life depends on it." And the line went dead.

Lindsey was speaking quietly into the cell phone, incandescently nude. Then she shook her head. "Not enough time. Shit! We should have had this number wired up in advance."

I stood up and pulled on some jeans and a sweatshirt. The house was quite cold, the way we keep it so my Arizona body heat doesn't smother Lindsey in bed beside me.

"What are you doing?"

"Going to the Jack in the Box down on McDowell, the pay phone. That's what he said to do. He'll call again."

"No way."

"I've got to, darling." I pulled on socks and laced up running shoes.

"I'm calling Kimbrough. Phoenix PD."

"Not enough time," I said, pulling on my black leather jacket. "Phoenix PD will fuck it up."

She turned off the phone. "Damn it!" she whispered.

I pulled the black nylon holster off the bedside table, checked to see the Python was loaded, and slid it securely into my belt.

Seven minutes later I rounded the corner onto McDowell, leaving behind the dark quiet of Willo. It was a little after three on Thursday morning, and traffic on McDowell was light. The red porch light of Fire Station 4 glowed in the dry, chilly air. Behind the glass doors, all the fire engines were home asleep. Across the street, a two-story inflatable gorilla looked down on me. He went with the pawn shop, which, in one of Phoenix's more tasteless ahistorical acts, occupied a building that had been a synagogue when I was a kid.

I walked quickly on McDowell. A Phoenix police cruiser flew by heading west, paying no attention to me. Up ahead, a couple of low-riders sat in the drive-in parking lot, steam coming out of their tailpipes. A large black kid in an Arizona Cardinals parka stood at the drive-through window ordering. As I walked into the cones of light I made out the pay phone at the edge of the lot, nobody around. I thought it was a fool's errand, but didn't know what else to do. Maybe Leo O'Keefe had been in prison so long he didn't realize these inner-city pay phones were rigged so they could only call out, to foil the drug trade.

But as I walked closer, it was ringing.

I sprinted the last fifteen feet and picked up a receiver that was chipped and sticky with grime.

"Mapstone," I said.

"Walk to the front of Kenilworth School. Come up the steps into the dark under the columns. Do it now."

I didn't even try to engage him. I hung up the phone, jogged across McDowell and headed west. At Fifth Avenue, I could see a figure in dark sweatshirt, hood up, hanging out at the Mexican shrimp cocktail shop: Lindsey. I keyed the auto-dial on my cell phone, still concealed in my pocket, and told her where I was going. I turned south at Burt Easley's Fun Shop and disappeared into the darkened neighborhood. I was aware of her behind me, but when I turned to look around me the sidewalk and street were empty.

Leo O'Keefe, in my neighborhood, on the steps of my grade school. At the press briefing, we had handed out the newest prison photo of him. We had explained our theory that he had come back to get revenge. Why, the press asked? Because he felt railroaded in the Guadalupe shooting, we said. Why now, the press pressed? Because the media coverage of Peralta winning the election had driven him to make a dramatic statement. It was a neat theory. It was the only one we had. But theory was running into reality in the cold desert night.

I walked down the sidewalks I had walked as a kid, dragging my way to school, flying home. Past the stately trunks of palm trees and the smart little World War I-era bungalows that had survived the coming of the underground freeway. Tonight they were all dark and silent, not even a dog to bark at a tall man in a leather jacket moving along at a half jog, half walk. Half a mile southeast of here the streets degenerated into a nasty mix of crack houses and young hustlers—the cops called it "Boys Town"—but up here I felt only solitude. If O'Keefe was nearby, I could only sense him in the aftertaste of my nightmare.

At Culver, the old school building loomed ahead. Barry Goldwater went to school there. Many years later, so did I. Now, as the constant low moan of traffic attested, it had an eight-lane freeway running beneath it. It was classic, columned and floodlighted against vandals. But, sure enough, gloom sat securely at the top of the front steps.

I spoke softly into my jacket. "I'm at Kenilworth, I'm going to the steps now."

Suddenly the trunk of a palm tree shattered beside me, and then came the deep boom and echo of a large-caliber weapon. I followed the shreds of palm tree down to the cold sidewalk, banging my knees and elbows. Rolling behind the tree trunk, I clung to the ground, my heart hammering against my ribs. I brought the Python up next to my face, resting the coolness of the barrel against my cheek. With my other hand, I pulled out the cell phone.

"Dave, Dave…"

"I'm OK. Don't come up." I scanned the school, the park, the darkened houses. Everything was still. The shot could have come from anywhere.

Lindsey said, "What was that noise?"

"Somebody took a shot at me with something very large."

"Can you get under cover?"

"I'm OK. Behind a palm tree at the northwest corner of Culver and Fifth Avenue."

Just then I saw a blur at the far end of the school steps. O'Keefe.

Instinct took over and I sprang up, crossing the old playground quickly, my magnum held in a combat grip, two-handed. I made it to the side of the building and fell against the wall. No shots came.

"We're on the move," I said into the phone. "Suspect is headed south from the school. Let them know he is being pursued by a plainclothes deputy!" I stuck the phone back in my pocket and sprang forward up the stairs. The gloomy area behind the columns was empty. But beyond, I caught a glimpse of a figure running hard out the other side of the playground.

He wasn't that fast. I took the steps down three at a time, my knees crying in protest. Then I dashed past swings and unidentifiable play equipment at a hard run. My lungs ached against the cold air, but I was gaining on him.

"Sheriff's deputy!" I yelled. "Stop! I am armed!"

I could make out a man in dark clothing and some kind of a baseball cap. He ran down the sidewalk, paused, then took off again running west toward Seventh Avenue. I put on the jets and got to within 100 yards of him when a pair of headlights shot up out of the earth and a horn screamed an angry klaxon.

He disappeared down the freeway onramp.

I went after him.

Suddenly we were in the tunnel. Interstate 10, the Papago Freeway, the mainline between Jacksonville, Florida, and Santa Monica, California, running like an underground river of metal and headlights. It smelled like catalytic converters and leaky oil and confined concrete. I made a fool's calculation and cut across the ramp just as a city garbage truck came through at battle speed. Then I reached the shoulder, hard against the tunnel wall, with nothing but a white line between me and the automotive age, going 80 miles an hour. The roar of engines and wheels was constant and deafening, even at this time of morning. To this white noise was added frantic honking at the fools running down the freeway. But I could see. The tunnel lights cast a strange arctic daylight. Car headlights shot past like comets from hell.

"We're in the freeway," I shouted into the phone. "Moving eastbound in the westbound lanes." The little digital display glowed happily back: "No service available."

I ran gingerly along the oily concrete as cars rocketed past. I lost sight of O'Keefe. Then I had him: bounding across the traffic lanes like a desperate squirrel.

Screeching tires cut above the noise, and suddenly there was a cascade of snaps and concussions, the odd sounds of metal and composite materials striking substantial objects at high speed. I looked toward the oncoming lanes and saw two cars collide trying to avoid the crazed man running toward them. Car parts abandoned ship and flew wildly into the thickening air. Metal scraped on the pavement, releasing showers of orange sparks too close to gas tanks. The two cars were spinning together, not slowly, and they were headed right for me.

I jammed my feet into place and forced my mental transmission into emergency reverse. It was maybe ten feet in the opposite direction to a little setback in the concrete wall, but it might as well have been 1,000 miles. My stomach filled with panic and bile. There was another sickening *screee! booff!* kind of sound as a third vehicle smashed into them from the rear. I didn't turn back to see. There wasn't time. The wall finally gave up a precious corner. I dived into it and prayed.

Chapter Ten

I was forty-three years old and in the principal's office. We all were. Me, Lindsey, Kimbrough, half a dozen Phoenix cops, and the school security guard who had opened the place so we had somewhere to sit. It was 4:45 a.m. on Thursday.

"Dave went to school here, and now he's the sheriff," Lindsey said to the security guard. "They ought to have a Dave Mapstone Day."

"Yes, ma'am," he said, trying to understand.

"Sheriff, if I may speak frankly," Kimbrough said.

"Yes, yes." I waved my hand at him. I was sitting bent over in a too-small plastic chair, suddenly wishing I could sleep for about a hundred years.

"Sir," Kimbrough said, "with all due respect."

Lindsey said, "Just say it. I bet I agree with it."

He let loose: "What the fuck"—this last word was shouted—"was that little stunt about!?" He added quietly, "Sheriff."

He wheeled on Lindsey. "And you! You were supposed to keep him from doing something pretty much just like this!"

"Sorry," she said. "He's headstrong. I like that, sometimes."

"Jesus!" he said. "It's like you have Peralta's recklessness without, without…"

He let it hang, and a grizzled Phoenix captain said, "His balls."

Kimbrough raised up and said, "Fuck you. Where were your people when we needed them? Where were those silly-ass bicycle patrols? The suspect just walks down Interstate 10 and gets away, while Phoenix PD is at Krispy Kreme."

Kimbrough turned back to me. "How did he even get your number?"

"It's listed," I said, feeling ever more foolish.

"Who's going to write this report?" a younger city cop demanded, realistically.

God, my head and knees hurt. Maybe I'd end up like one of those old people who has total knee replacement with some very expensive composite material, kind of like the stuff flying off those cars in the tunnel, and yet your knees still hurt like hell.

I looked around the room. *A jurisdictional goat-fuck*, I heard Peralta's voice say. Yes, my friend, and you would know just how to take charge. Just the right amount of politicking, and just the right amount of hard-ass. Well, if I knew those things I'd have tenure at a major university history department.

I said quietly, "It's not O'Keefe." Everybody stopped talking and looked at me.

"O'Keefe didn't shoot Peralta."

"Oh, bullshit," the Phoenix captain said under his breath.

"He just tried to shoot you, too!" Kimbrough said. "And from the way you describe the shot, I wouldn't be surprised if ballistics finds this is the same gun that shot Peralta."

I shook my head. "He's not our guy."

"Oh, Jesus Christ!" Kimbrough said. "Leo O'Keefe was an accessory in the worst assault on Maricopa County deputies in history. Leo O'Keefe is a convicted murderer. Now, he's an escapee. We have a threatening note, sent by him, found on the body of a former deputy, who was also involved in that Guadalupe incident. And now he's tried to take a whack at you, Mapstone—you, the deputy who arrested him and signed his booking record. The guy is two decades of trouble. He's a monster."

I had to admit told that way it sounded airtight. Leo O'Keefe, broken out of the big house and come to settle the big score with the sheriff's office. But I also knew the ways of law enforcement bureaucracies. Leo was our only theory in a high-profile shooting. Without Leo, we were screwed.

I said, "It wasn't a threatening note. It was his name on a piece of paper. Tonight, Leo didn't seem to know who I was, beyond the guy on the television from the press conference yesterday. That doesn't sound like somebody who's been carrying a hit list stamped on his heart since 1979. He said he didn't shoot Peralta."

Lindsey said, "Dave, can you really believe what he said on the phone? Did he actually say he didn't shoot Peralta?"

"It's not just that," I said. "It's Nixon. He didn't know about Nixon turning up dead."

"What...?" Kimbrough started.

It was true. We had held back the information of Dean Nixon's murder from the media. In yesterday's press briefing on the hunt for Peralta's killer, we didn't even mention Nixon.

For one thing, it was a piece of critical information that would hold down the number of needy nutcases who might come in and confess in O'Keefe's place. If Nixon's murder were tied to the shooting of Peralta, then the real killer would know that information. And holding it back would have kept the suspect off balance, if he thought we hadn't discovered Nixon's body yet—if the two shootings were connected. Plus, cops just liked to hoard information.

But O'Keefe didn't know that Dean Nixon was dead.

"He asked me if I had talked to Dean Nixon. As in, present tense."

Kimbrough pursed his lips, said nothing.

"Maybe he was just messing with you," said another city cop. She was sipping on some coffee in Styrofoam cups that had appeared from the security guard. I waved one away.

"Maybe," I said. "But why?"

The captain said, "To lure you out. Make you do pretty much what you did. Only O'Keefe wasn't a good enough shot. Hell, he didn't even finish off Peralta."

We sat in silence. The room smelled of Lysol and chalk dust. I wished Peralta were here to dispense with this PD bastard. Younger cops began the real work: writing up the incident report.

Another cop—she looked like a tougher Jennifer Aniston—said, "Your guy, I'll say this about him. Whether he's the killer or not, he was willing to run into the busiest freeway in town to get away from talking about it."

"This is nuts!" the captain said. "If he didn't fire that shot, who the hell did?"

"Somebody," I said, "who didn't want him talking to me."

Two hours later, Lindsey and I sat over breakfast at Susan's, a diner out on Glendale Avenue. It was one of Peralta's favorite places, and it served terrific comfort food. I also sought comfort in the newspaper. So while Lindsey fiddled with her Palm Pilot, I ate scrambled eggs and read the *Republic*. Peralta's shooting had moved off the front page, replaced by a thumbsucker on a huge new development north of the city. Why did they call them "master-planned communities," these endless tracts of houses without even a park or a neighborhood drugstore? I recalled the line about the Holy Roman Empire being neither holy, nor Roman, nor an empire. Then I moved onto a helping of requisite Valley crime stories: A New York gang boss was found running a drug ring in the Phoenix suburbs. A landscape worker fed himself and his brand-new fiancée into a wood chipper. A woman stopped to help a pair of stranded motorists with a baby, who turned out to be robbers and shot her dead. My hometown.

"Dave." Lindsey reached past the ketchup and hot sauce, taking my hand.

She locked those twilight blue eyes on me intensely. "I really need you to stay safe," she whispered, and her eyes watered over with tears. "Please, Dave..."

I squeezed her hand back, feeling guilty and responsible. I was about to say something sappy when Kimbrough appeared at the front window, nodded awkwardly, then came in the door.

I waved him over to the table. He was wearing jeans and a plaid shirt, his gun and badge prominently on his belt. He had an evidence envelope in his hand.

"We haven't seen you in ages," Lindsey said, wiping her face and commencing to rip apart the interior of a grapefruit with her fork. Kimbrough pulled up a chair, exchanged pleasantries with Susan, and ordered coffee.

He swallowed the lava-like liquid without flinching. Cops and coffee. I would never understand it.

"David, I was out of line back there," he said. "I apologize."

"You weren't out of line," I said. "I was a dumb fuck. I just didn't know what to do."

He shuffled in the chair, ran a hand over the smooth, dark globe of his scalp. I said, "Don't worry about it, E.J." I had never called him by his first name before.

He nodded, sipped more coffee, and relaxed a bit. "We have news," he said. He slid the evidence container onto the table. Through the clear plastic, I could see a manila envelope, faded with age. On the front, written in a scratchy hand, was: "To be opened in the event of my death."

"Where did you get this?"

"Nixon's ex-wife," Kimbrough said. "A woman named Joyce Bellman, who lives in Tempe. You know her?"

"Nope,' I said. "Nixon was single when I knew him."

"Well, she's wife number two out of three," Kimbrough said. "We tracked her down this morning on a next-of-kin notification. She said he left this envelope with her years ago. When I saw what she had, I figured you'd want to see it."

It felt light and unremarkable in my hand. I set it back on the table.

"Have you opened it?"

He shook his head.

"Got any gloves?"

He reached in his pocket and pulled out some latex gloves. I slipped them on and opened the evidence container.

"Everyone will witness the chain of custody is secure," I said. "I don't want to be lectured by some Phoenix PD asshole twice in the same day."

I undid the clasp and the flap opened with no resistance. I slid in a finger and dilated the envelope so we could see inside. It was another envelope, slightly smaller. I gently slid it out. On the front, written in a firmer hand, it said: "For the U.S. Attorney Only."

Kimbrough and Lindsey looked at each other.

"Dean Nixon reaches out from the grave," I said. "But why wouldn't that information be on the cover envelope?"

"Maybe Nixon assumed his ex would be the one to open the outside envelope if he died," Lindsey said.

I paused and weighed it in my hand. The gloves made my fingers sweat.

"What should we do?" Lindsey said. Our breakfasts sat unattended, getting cold.

"I guess let the feds know," I said. But now I was feeling awake and curious. "But we can examine the evidence, of course."

Kimbrough smiled broadly. "Of course."

"We don't suspect a federal crime has occurred, do we?" I asked.

"Not us," they said in unison.

"But this does pertain to an active murder investigation," I said.

"Very active," Lindsey said.

"Then let's see what Dean was afraid of all those years ago."

I undid the clasp, but the envelope was also sealed. I worked the flap open as gently as I could, and the aging glue gave way with reluctance. Inside was a thick wad of paper. It was stuck inside so tightly that it resisted being pulled out. I could make out colors, lines, grids.

It was a map.

Chapter Eleven

We didn't have far to go. The map, a detailed plat from the U.S. Geological Survey, showed the area around Shaw Butte in the North Mountain Preserve. It highlighted a trail in yellow marker, then diverged to what the map said was an abandoned mine shaft. Next to that, in a precise hand, were instructions on how to find Dean Nixon's buried treasure.

We walked up the trail armed with a shovel, crime-scene tape, and more evidence containers from the trunk of Kimbrough's unmarked Crown Victoria. Ahead of us were bare sunbaked mountains that once cradled the northern edge of the city, marking the beginning of the desert wilderness. Now the city had run around them. But somehow Phoenix had mustered the momentary courage to save the mountains themselves from development. Today we passed a handful of hikers, but the preserve was mostly deserted on a weekday.

As we walked, Kimbrough talked about his family. One child, a boy, was six now, and another was on the way in June. His wife had left the County Attorney's Office—they met when she was a prosecutor—and she was going to set up her own family law practice. This was Kimbrough's fifteenth year with the Sheriff's Office. He was five years younger than me, and came here from the Drug Enforcement Administration when the former sheriff, also a DEA man, won election.

"Now I know why I like you," I said. "You're an outsider in this department like me."

"That and we have great taste in clothes." He laughed.

We walked up a well prepared trail, but it was still work. The hard desert ground was defined by loose rocks, sand, and outcroppings of jumping cactus. I felt every foot of elevation in my knees and calves. But as we kept walking, the pain lessened, as did the immediate memory of the gunshot that made me dive for the sidewalk just a few hours before.

"Luckily the snakes are hibernating in winter," I said.

"Great," Kimbrough said.

"'Course it's been a warm winter, Dave," Lindsey said.

As we neared the summit and left the trail, the ugliness of the day became evident. A weather inversion had clamped the smog down hard on the city, just like the lid on a bowl. Only Phoenix's bowl was the purple and brown necklace of mountains that surrounded it. From where we stood, we should have been able to see the soaring blue towers of the Sierra Estrella to the south and the sheer expanse of the White Tanks to the west. Both were gone, replaced by a yellow-brown haze that spread out across the desert floor. Even Squaw Peak and Camelback, much closer, were barely visible. To the south, the Sunnyslope section of the city fell away in a series of rooftops, palm trees, and billboards until it, too, disappeared in the muck. The line of skyscrapers on the Central Corridor shimmered and faded. To the north, Moon Valley and Deer Valley, newer parts of Phoenix, sprawled around Lookout Mountain, itself cloaked in brown air.

"Yuck," Lindsey said. We were all winded from the climb, and the sight of the air didn't make breathing easier.

"I remember when the sky here was the bluest blue in the world," I said, working my way up a slick boulder. "But I'm sounding like an old fogey."

Lindsey grabbed my hand and pulled herself up on the next level of rock. "You're a young fogey," she said, "like me."

We paused and studied the map. Sure enough, a slab of concrete was set into a cluster of boulders, marked off by signs that warned "Danger. Abandoned Mine."

"I didn't realize there was mining in the Valley," Lindsey said, kindly teasing my eternal pedagogic sensibility.

"Yeah, my wife thinks these mountains just look like giant slag heaps," Kimbrough said. "But she's from Pennsylvania."

"Well, these mountains were really not much. The mining districts east of here, around Globe, or north in the Bradshaw Mountains actually had some gold and silver." I restrained myself. "Anyway, there were a few mines around Phoenix. Squaw Peak had some quicksilver mines. A German POW hid in one for awhile when he escaped, back in World War II."

I could go on all day, and Lindsey said my history talks were wildly romantic. But we fell silent as we studied Nixon's instructions. Northeast corner of the concrete slab, right by the fence pole. I stuck the shovel in the hard, dry dirt and started digging.

After several cuts at the ground, I was about to let Kimbrough take his turn digging. Then the blade of the shovel struck metal.

"That's it," I said. I changed the angle of the shovel and soon outlined what looked like an old metal ammunition box, just the size of a bread box, its olive green paint suddenly peeking out of the blond and gray desert soil.

"Whatever it was," Lindsey said, "Nixon didn't want it at his trailer. But he didn't want it that far away, either."

I grasped the handle of the box and pulled it out of the ground. "Well, we're about to find out."

I put latex gloves back on and released the metal catch on the ammo box. The top swung open, releasing sand and rocks. Inside it was empty.

"I don't believe it," Kimbrough said. "This is like when Geraldo opened Al Capone's vault."

"Wait a minute." I put my hand on the bottom and it gave way. A piece of dark metal, cut to create a false bottom. I pulled out the metal plate and beneath it was some kind of book, wrapped in plastic. I pulled it out and shook it off, being paranoid about scorpions and other desert creepy-crawlies. But inside it was clean and dry, a red, hardcover journal. It was the kind of logbook you might have seen in any small business a generation ago.

"Hmmmm," Kimbrough said, reacting to the cover. It was a vivid cartoon of two pigs in police uniforms, having sex while riding a Harley. Beneath it was inscribed, "MCSD RIVER HOGS."

"That dates it," I said. "Back in the seventies, it was the Maricopa County Sheriff's *Department*, MCSD, when we were trying to prove how big-city we were."

"What were the River Hogs?" Lindsey asked.

I shook my head, looking over at Kimbrough.

"Before my time," he said. "But I never heard the phrase before."

"When did Nixon's ex get that envelope?" I asked.

"She didn't recall exactly," he said. "They divorced in 1991, and she moved to Tempe. She knows Nixon gave her the envelope to hang onto after they divorced. She said she hadn't even seen Nixon since 1995."

"Dave's ex gave him a BMW," Lindsey said, poking my ribs.

"So he was anticipating somebody killing him for at least five years, maybe longer?" I said.

"Maybe," Kimbrough said. "But he was a drunk and a washout as a law enforcement officer. Maybe he was just paranoid." I held out the book again and opened the cover. Beyond some blank initial sheets, the pages turned dense with columns. Pages and pages of numbers and columns. I flipped through. Nothing but numbers and columns. One column appeared to be dates, starting in 1977. On the last page, the date was 12/31/80. Another column was clearly about money: Each page saw that column set off with a precisely-drawn dollar sign—and the same person appeared to have written all the entries. The sums weren't small, $1,000 being a common amount, and some lines showing as high as $15,000.

"What's that?" Kimbrough indicated another column, with four-digit numbers.

I shook my head. "Some kind of code, maybe." I scanned the pages, and the four-digit numbers frequently repeated themselves. A few appeared quite regularly, every week.

"Like a book-making operation?" Lindsey asked. I shook my head, feeling suddenly like something cold had wrapped itself around my neck.

"Or payoffs," I said. "Bribes to cops. Nixon left nothing in this case except this book. He obviously thought it was self-evident, and that the information was explosive. We're not talking about records of poker games, here."

"That's why he wrote the thing about taking it to the U.S. Attorney," Kimbrough said.

"So what is the code?" Lindsey asked. "Maybe there's a key somewhere in the book."

Kimbrough's star and gun hanging on his belt caught my eye, and it was clear. "They're badge numbers," I said.

Lindsey drew closer. "Jeez, Dave, are you in there?"

"What was Nixon's badge number?" I asked. Kimbrough shook his head.

"Hang on," Lindsey said, pulling out her Palm Pilot.

"I guess I have to get one of those," I said.

"This one's old," she said, using a stylus to make some marks on the little screen. "It takes a long time to beam into the mainframe down on Madison Street."

I looked out, past the blown-apart, burned boulders, over the brown haze obscuring the city. *Badge numbers.* So this was what Nixon wanted someone to see in the event of his death. Leo O'Keefe? No, Dean Nixon had been fearing something for a very long time, and it had to do with badge numbers.

"Got it," Lindsey said, reading out Nixon's number from the central computer. And, sure enough, Nixon was a regular in the book. In just one month, he accounted for $8,500, and that was 1979 money.

Lindsey drew close to me and began scanning the pages herself. Suddenly, she drew in a sharp breath. "Oh!"

I couldn't believe it. Didn't want to. But there it was. And it reappeared. Again and again, on page after page.

"That can't be," I said.

"What the hell are you guys talking about," Kimbrough demanded. But then his eyes picked up the four digits, too.

"Oh, my God," he said.

There was only one badge number that was so familiar in the Sheriff's Office that everyone knew it by sight.

Chapter Twelve

As acting sheriff of Maricopa County, I could tell you a lot about what we do. We have 1,500 sworn deputies, and a volunteer posse of 3,200 reserve deputies. We police a county spread over 9,200 square miles, a larger area than some states. On the side of our patrol cars is the motto: "Protect and serve."

The Sheriff's Office is organized into nine bureaus. Patrol and detective operations are handled in four districts, dividing up the county. We have expensive and showy helicopters, heavily armed SWAT teams, and even a tank. We have a low-rider to win friends in the barrio.

Detaining prisoners is a big part of what we do. They're kept in six different jails, including the former sheriff's fabled Tent City jail, where the inmates live in tents, wear pink underwear, and eat green baloney. They seem to enjoy it.

Fifteen deputies have been killed in the line of duty, starting in 1922.

But that's all numbers and organization, gadgets and background material off the sheriff's web site. I know. I helped write it. But it doesn't get at the heart and character of the organization. Even college faculties have heart and character. At the MCSO, even under the former sheriff's showbiz years, those traits were best expressed, and embodied, in a man named Peralta.

I knew all his bad sides. He was stubborn. He could be relentless. He was the very antithesis of the teary-communicative, huggy-therapeutic postmodern man. But I had been blessed by his brave heart and manly charity more times than I could count. Not just the night in Guadalupe when he saved my life, but in the aftermath of the shooting when he made sure I was assigned to easy duty. He would have been insulted if I had thanked him. To his mind, I had done my duty, and that wrapped me forever in his web of mutual obligation. That's why he stayed in touch all those years when we had nothing in common but a shared past. And it's why he gave me a job when nobody else would, and kept the Jack Abernathys of the department off my back until I had time to prove myself. That was Peralta.

But right then he lay before me unseeing, unhearing, a machine doing his breathing. We were alone in the room. I sat deeply in a chair with slick vinyl sides, watching his chest rise. I was in quite a state. But no one would know. Only Lindsey would, but she had gone with Kimbrough to log in the evidence we found in Dean Nixon's ammo box. They figured I would be OK alone here, guarded by a phalanx of deputies in jumpsuits and flak jackets patrolling the hospital halls.

"Log the evidence in quietly for now," I'd instructed Kimbrough. He'd looked at me pointedly. "What are you asking me to do, Sheriff?"

I said, "I am asking you to do just what I said. That's all."

And then I came to Good Sam to sit with the man whose badge number appeared repeatedly in Dean Nixon's logbook next to large amounts of cash.

I'm a good man to have in a crisis. The high-functioning child who grew up around old people, "man child" Grandmother called me. The multitalented adult who could do all sorts of different things well, but could never quite succeed at any of them. The cop who was too smart for law enforcement. The professor not smart enough to get tenure, or conform to the new political conventions of the academy, or even write popular history books that would sell.

And now, through a strange collision of events, all these destinies had been placed in my hands. Right that moment, my hands shook. My heart clubbed my ribcage. The point of pain between the belly and my heart had grown into a persistent ache.

"What have we gotten into?" I said to the mountain in the bed before me.

Only the mechanical wheeze of the respirator responded.

My voice was a dull monotone in a dim room. "Why is your badge number on those pages?"

I was suddenly so tired and angry with him, for putting me in this situation, for getting hurt, for abandoning us—it wasn't rational, but, as I say, I was in a state. Just as quickly, I filled with remorse. But finally, I came back around to Dean Nixon's record book, and the terrible history it gave. Could it possibly be true?

It would all have to go to Internal Affairs, of course. And to the feds. And to the media.

I had a lot of complaints and crotchets about the Sheriff's Office over the years. But I never, even at my most discontent, thought we were corrupt.

Maybe this was all some kind of put-on.

But if so, why did my stomach hurt so damned much?

I could not accept that this man before me was a dirty cop. I could not. I owed him my life, on more than one occasion. But a voice inside me, a voice trained by an unfaithful wife and a career ruined by betrayal, said, How well do we really know anyone, especially the people we love? And the voice of a trained historian, who knew to look beneath the surface, to view institutions skeptically, to distrust one's preconceptions…well, that voice told me I was in too deep.

"David?"

It was Sharon. She had come in silently and now stood behind me. I stood and gave her a quick hug.

"Have you been crying?" she asked.

It was a slander. It was the smog. I said, "You went back to the radio show?"

"I had to find a routine," she said. "Better to deal with other people's problems than mine." She was wearing expensive-looking cream slacks and a black blouse. Her black hair was pulled back in a ponytail, bringing out her high cheekbones. She sat in the other chair and took my hand.

"He won't wake up, David," she said. "I don't know what to do. I've read whole books and web sites on head trauma and comas, but it's shocking how little they know, even today. So much of it seems out of our hands."

She stood and worked her way around his bed, inspecting gauges, connections, fluids, contraptions. "We've been taking shifts, the girls and I. We try to have someone with him every moment they'll let us."

Peralta's color looked all wrong. His broad, expressive face—the turbulent synthesis of Aztecs and conquistadors—was several shades lighter than I had ever seen it. The crinkles around his eyes seemed etched in pink blood.

"David, how is the hunt going for this convict?"

"Badly," I said. "But I don't think he's our suspect anyway." I told her of the events of the past few hours, cleaning it up for civilian sensibilities, leaving out the part about the gunshot aimed at my head.

She shook her head with increasing agitation. "I can't believe someone can try to kill the sheriff of one of the largest counties in America, and you people are so helpless!"

"It's not that," I said quietly, feeling pretty damned helpless. "We're making progress. But it's taking us in a different direction."

"But David, you have a note pointing to this..."

"Leo O'Keefe."

"What a name," she said. "No wonder he's deranged. I'm going to write a book someday about what parents do to their children with rotten names."

"I'm not saying he's not involved. I'm just saying I don't think he pulled the trigger." I let silence fill in the room again. I had to talk to her. I just didn't know how.

"How is Lindsey? That is a pretty name."

"She's OK," I said. "She's concerned."

"Sometimes," Sharon said, "she reminds me of a young Susan Sontag, all that dark hair, and that poetic watchfulness she has."

"Different politics," I said. But I liked the phrase "poetic watchfulness." I added, "And she doesn't consider herself an intellectual. She's quite stubborn about that. But she is a great mind and soul."

"I like Lindsey," Sharon said, turning aside my idealistic parry. "I've come to like her. She's knocked off a lot of her rough edges the past couple of years."

"She's knocked off some of mine, too."

"I suppose so," Sharon said. "You certainly seem happy around her. I don't know if that's a reason to get married. Who said a second marriage is 'the triumph of hope over experience'?"

"Dr. Johnson," I said.

She patted my hand. "David, the Renaissance man. I hope she gets that about you."

"She does," I said. "She reads. We read to each other. That's a big deal today." I felt uncomfortable, as if I were defending Lindsey from a subtle, professionally engineered attack.

"You know," she said, "the day he was shot, I was wrapping up an article about women and marriage."

"Oh, yeah?" I was relieved for a slight change of subject.

"The headline, I guess, is that marriage is bad for women's growth. That's the way I see it." She sighed heavily. "I was trying to figure out how I was going to tell him about this without setting him off. How screwed up is that?"

"It sounds pretty bleak," I said. "About marriage."

"Oh, there are always exceptions, I guess. But in my line, love gone wrong is the biggest source of people's unhappiness. On the radio show, I could take nothing but lovelorn calls. I have the screener keep a better balance with other pathologies, just so I don't get bored."

She added quietly, "I haven't been sure I wanted to be married for years. Many women are that way, David. They're stunted in their growth taking care of their men."

She went on: "I can't say it quite like that on the radio, of course. It would disappoint the love fantasies of too many listeners, and their advertisers. So this article is for an academic journal. Publish or perish, you know all about that." She paused. "Anyway, I guess I should feel terribly guilty in the wake of all that's happened. So you and Lindsey have set a date? You're going to do this for a second time, David?"

There was a lot I wanted to say. But I just said, "April 30th. Central Methodist Church. We expect you both to be there."

She just smiled and nodded. Then, quietly, "David, I always imagined you as the scholar, just living the life of the mind."

I made myself talk. "Sharon, have you ever heard of something called the River Hogs?"

She said she hadn't, and asked the inevitable "why." I avoided answering, the cop way, by firing another question.

"What do you remember about Mike after the Guadalupe shooting? What was his state of mind?"

"His state of mind?" She laughed. "You were his partner, David. You tell me. You knew him better than I did, certainly back then." She smiled to herself. "You were such an oddity. This intense young man who read books and seemed gentle and thoughtful, among all these cowboys. I think I learned something about Mike from the way he gravitated to you, in spite of himself. It was like you filled a part of his soul that came from his father. It was a part he'd never let me into."

I sat up and rearranged myself, trying to find a comfortable perch in the chair. But there was nothing wrong with the chair.

I went on, "What was his life like off-duty? Did he talk about work?"

"He barely talked at all," she said, her huge eyes darkening.

"Did he have buddies he hung out with? Acquaintances? Anybody else he might have been talking to during that time."

I had thrown her out of synch. A rigid silence overcame her usual easy poise. "We were going through a hard time then," she said.

I plunged ahead heedlessly. "How so?"

She sighed and her fine cheeks flushed. "He had been having an affair."

My face must have given me away. She said, "You didn't know? I thought partners knew everything, certainly more than spouses. Oh, yes. It was some waitress at Hobo Joe's. Her name was Lisa. She was nineteen and had fake red hair. I blamed myself, of course. All women do."

I thought, Gosh, my ex-wife blamed me when she had affairs.

Sharon said, "I learned a hell of a lot about her, Lisa."

"What was her last name?"

"Cardiff. Lisa Ann Cardiff. Doesn't that sound like some porn star's name? Maybe I'm being too harsh. She was just a dumb kid, overwhelmed by his…What do you call it? Not charm. You're charming, David. But he's like this tidal wave of personality. So maybe Lisa was kind of like me, just flooded by him. I don't know how the hell he afforded her, on a sergeant's salary, when he had two daughters and I was trying to put myself through school…"

"I'm sorry," I said.

"Life is complicated," she said, looking over at her husband, lying two feet away, lost to the coma world. "He's not a bad man."

"No," I said.

And for a long time we sat, not speaking, barely breathing. Sharon and I were old friends. Our relationship had an ambiguousness that I had never dared explore. Now a new tension rippled through the room like the pulses from the monitors beside Peralta's bed.

Finally, she said, "I have this feeling that I don't want to know what all these questions have to do with here and now. And yet, David, I know you are about to tell me."

Chapter Thirteen

The midafternoon sun broke through the smog, sending intense sunbeams into the little study that sat just off the living room. When my grandparents built the house back in the 1920s, this room was Grandfather's office and behind it was the examination room where he plied his dental practice. That didn't last. By the time I was living in the house, the exam room had long since been turned into an enclosed sunporch, which it still was, facing the interior courtyard and garden. But the office still had traces of Grandfather in the big, cherry desk and leather swivel chair. I swear I could still get a whiff of his cigars. Peralta smoked cigars.

Now the office was half filled with my books and papers, and half occupied by Lindsey's two laptop computers, hardcover Russian novels, and a collection of Mexican Day of the Dead art. The figures now gaily stared at me, skulls and bones, as I sat alone behind the old desk. Lindsey would be back with lunch and Starbucks, soon. She had left a weapon at my feet, just in case. It was a light, lethal Heckler & Koch submachine gun. I wondered what Grandfather would say to see this device in the well of his beloved desk. The H&K wasn't much of a companion for a life of the mind.

I needed time to think, time for sober reflection, as one of my professors used to say. Actually, I badly wanted a martini, or some scotch neat. I settled for a Diet Coke and the Bud Powell CD on the stereo. Powell was all wrong for my mood, assertively innovative, confidently modern, string bass and piano exploring new combinations far from the world of cops and mortals. But I let it be.

It wasn't that I hated the stereotype of the absentminded professor, thinking tiny great thoughts while running into doors. It was that I never took it personally. I was engaged, worldly, even carnal—that was what the women in my life had said, and I took it as an accurate assessment. But the realization was pushing me deeper into the leather chair: A whole world had been going on around me twenty years before, and I had been...oblivious.

Peralta was having an affair. Of course he was. Little things made sense now. But I only realized it as Sharon was telling me, decades later. Maybe he was having more than an affair. What else didn't I know?

Dean Nixon was apparently the bookkeeper for some sinister enterprise. Badge numbers and money and dates. Who the hell were the River Hogs? I had spent nearly four years out in the patrol districts, accepted as one of the go-to deputies, but I had never heard the phrase. What else didn't I know?

And now Peralta was lying wounded, perhaps mortally. Dean had been murdered in the most squalid circumstances. That kid I booked years before had broken out of prison, trying desperately to contact me. And someone else was out there, trying to stop him through the barrel of a gun.

The only event in common was that shooting in Guadalupe. But even that didn't explain Peralta's cryptic reminder: "Mapstone—Camelback Falls."

What else didn't I know?

How much of an excuse is youth?

I was young, oh my God, was I young. But I was a quick study of routines and skills. Knowledge of history and some innate intuition gave me judgment beyond my years, especially rare for the late 1960s and 1970s. Adults loved me. When my peers were sowing wild oats, I was working as a deputy sheriff, seeing things most people didn't even realize existed.

And I was also carrying a backbreaking class load in graduate school. I was so unfashionable. A narc in class, a pig on campus. Out on the job, I was the outcast who had to hide my books, conceal my degree, tell my insights into the human condition only to myself.

My one real girlfriend left me for a rich doctor with a sailboat.

By the time I was in my mid-twenties, I felt so old, so experienced—in some ways so world weary. Maybe, I realized, that was one thing that had attracted me to Lindsey three years before. I saw something of myself in her.

But there was a shadow world I was beginning to see.

After I had left Peralta, I called Kimbrough and walked him through what I wanted done. We would go by the book. Nothing less, but nothing more. Internal Affairs would be brought in, with no interference from me or anyone else. Our liaison officer with the FBI and U.S. Attorney would brief the feds on what we had uncovered. I would make a courtesy call to the county supervisors, county attorney, and state attorney general. And we would not talk to the media, not yet.

I asked him, "Do you agree?"

He laughed sadly through his nose. "That doesn't matter, Sheriff. It's going to blow up on us, and we're all going to be within the blast radius."

The front door opened, and Lindsey came in with a cardboard Starbucks carrier and takeout from the China Doll. I got up and helped her carry things. Then I took her in my arms, full body close against full body, and held her for a long time.

⟨⟩⟨⟩⟨⟩

The dinner crowd was gathering at Durant's as we slid into the cool slickness of a dark red banquette. I had changed into a charcoal Brooks Brothers suit, and Lindsey was wearing a smashing little black dress. We both enjoyed dress-up, and Durant's was only one degree separated from the very adult 1950s, when it was one of two or three restaurants in town. Now, it rode the wave of retro nostalgia and pervasive irony. No cell phones in Durant's. The only thing that didn't quite fit was the darkly good-looking man who awaited us. His name was Bobby Hamid.

He had already made a show of kissing Lindsey's hand when we came in. Now he sat, perfectly tailored in a priceless gray suit, dazzling us with his smile.

"Miss Lindsey," he said. "Now I understand Dr. Mapstone's obsession with you all these years."

"And I understand Sheriff Peralta's obsession with you," she said, smiling sweetly.

He sat back with mock horror and smiled again. "Oh, Dr. Mapstone, are American women not the most delightful creatures in the world? Full of spunk and vinegar. There are more descriptive words in Persian, but I won't bore you."

We ordered drinks. Bobby wanted a kir royale, and instructed the waiter meticulously on its construction. I settled for a Bombay Sapphire martini, straight up, one olive.

Bobby was full of pleasantries and solicitations, asking about Peralta, giving me best wishes at such a trying time for the Sheriff's Office. Peralta had only spent the past fifteen years trying to put Bobby in prison forever. I had been close enough to see that Bobby's elegance masked a cruel gangster, a man who rose from an Iranian exchange student to become one of the richest men in Phoenix. Bobby's American dream had been paid for with drugs, prostitution, and murder. But he was undeniably charming, and not with the bad-boy musk of criminals. No, Bobby was a learned man, a cultured man. He gave to all the right local charities. Once he had saved my life.

"I don't understand why you didn't want to come here," he was saying as the drinks arrived. "Durant's is a Phoenix institution. Grown-up. Classy. Fully of history. Just like you, Professor. Or, I should say, Sheriff."

"Well, Bobby, I guess it was a reluctance for the media to see the acting sheriff having dinner with a disreputable character like you."

His lips maintained their curl of amusement but a flush crept into his fine cheeks. "What is the country song? 'All my rowdy friends have settled down.' That is why I have kept my distance as you took over as sheriff. People would not understand. But, Dr. Mapstone, you called me this afternoon, remember? You may be ashamed of me, but I know you need me."

And he was right.

"Bobby, you used to own that place down in the riverbed, Terry's Swedish Message Institute, right?"

Bobby sampled his kir royale. "Very nice," he said. "Do you know the Ayatollah Khomeini spent years in Paris before coming back to ruin Persia? Me, I would have stayed in Paris..." He sipped again. "Why are you asking me this?"

Lindsey said, "He's calculating whether various statutes of limitations have run out."

Bobby ignored her. He leaned forward on the table and fixed me in his black eyes.

"David, you are starting to acquire some of Chief Peralta's quirks, no? This fascination with character assassination. Combined with your fixation on the past. If I had ever owned Terry's"—he sipped again—"that would have been many years ago. Back in the era of disco in America and revolution in my homeland."

He reached forward quickly, and I could sense Lindsey tense her arm toward the holster concealed on her right thigh. But he only wanted bread. He broke off a piece and daintily buttered it, careful to set his knife at a precise angle on the bread plate.

"Did you see the profile of me in *Fortune* last month?" he asked. "They called me 'the venture capitalist to know in Arizona.' I thought real estate had been good to me. That was nothing until I gave these software developers a few million. Oh, the New Economy, I love it."

I said, "Well, if you had owned Terry's Swedish Message Institute—just hypothetically speaking—I imagine you would have run across the name 'River Hogs.'"

The waiter reappeared and we ordered dinner. This would be an interesting expense to walk through the department's financial services bureau. After the man went away, Bobby regarded me with something new in his eyes.

"You know, David, the essence of dramatic irony is conveyed by the play *Oedipus Rex*. The king searches for a truth that the audience already knows will destroy him. That kind of investigation can be quite dangerous."

I sipped my martini. Bobby liked to talk.

"River Hogs," he said. "I have not heard that name for many years. Not since I..." A flock of snowbirds went past on the way to a table, a flash of pink and green and laughter. Back home in New Jersey the landscape was gray and the temperature was in the 20s.

"And?" Lindsey said.

"Let me ask you a question, David," he said. "Where have you heard this name? Why is this important to you now?"

"It's connected to a major investigation," I said. "You know I can't say more."

He sat back and nodded his head. "Of course."

"The River Hogs," I prompted.

"Well, David, they were your people," he said. "The River Hogs was a gang of deputies."

"Maricopa County deputies?"

He nodded.

"And this was, what, a pinochle club?"

Bobby shook his head, lightly jostling his movie-star hair. It was starting to go gray, which made him look even better.

"That was a long time ago," he said. "But one heard things. And they were not good. The River Hogs offered protection to certain kinds of businesses, in exchange for certain kinds of, let us say, reciprocity."

I reached for my drink too fast. "This is absurd. I worked in the East County patrol district."

"David, you asked me," he said. He paused, then added, "Now you know why my relationship with the police has always been so—what is the right word?—textured."

"Then why didn't I ever hear about these rogue deputies?" I demanded.

He said, "Maybe we moved in different circles."

I realized my shoulders were rigid bars against the banquette. I made myself lower them, relax. "Are these people, these deputies, still in business?"

"I would not know that," he said. "And, because I know you will ask, let me emphasize that I heard things, only that, I made it a point never to know more, and never to know the identity of individuals. It seemed like the way to maintain a healthy lifestyle."

After dinner, I just had to drive. I launched the BMW into the river of headlights flowing east on Camelback Road, and we passed 7th Street, 16th, 24th, headed in the direction of Scottsdale. It was definitely high season, the streets crowded with tags from Ohio, Ontario, Minnesota, New York, and Massachusetts, and Arizona tags on the kinds of cars so bland that they could only exist in the fleets of rental-car companies. Lindsey held my hand and we took comfort in the alchemy of silence and city lights.

"I turned the log over to Internal Affairs," I said as we missed the signal at 44th Street.

"What else could you do, Dave?"

I just shook my head. "I didn't even want to know who else was in the book. There's such a thing as due process. Even if this stopped twenty years ago, we've got evidence that could tarnish good cops. Who the hell was Dean Nixon? A bad cop. I owe it to everybody to make sure we do this right."

"You sound like you're trying to convince yourself."

"Maybe it's not badge numbers," I said, not believing it. "Maybe it's something else."

"Partial zip codes?"

I took a left at Arcadia Drive. The oleanders and citrus trees gave way to the arched mass of Camelback Mountain, sitting blacker than the night sky, directly ahead. The road began to rise.

"I need to stay out of this and let IA do its job. The feds might get involved, too. I just need to stand aside."

"But you won't," Lindsey said quietly, proudly.

Arcadia made a hard right, turning into a street called Valle Vista Road. Off behind us you could see why. The city lights expanded grandly behind us, an electric empire flowing out to the far mountains.

"Oh, I love this view," she said, turning in her seat to take it in. Her hair glowed darkly in the reflected light.

I came to a closed gate, immersed in rock and hedges. The car sighed into park. "This should be it."

"What is it, Dave? Your old college make-out spot?"

"Look." I pointed through the landscaping to a modish adobe house perched out on a crag. "It's Camelback Falls."

"Wow. Pretty cool spot. Doesn't look like anyone's home." The house was as dark as the street was deserted. "Do you know who owns it now?"

"No. I just wanted to see it. In a way, this is the last message I have from Peralta."

The city twinkled back at us. Across the Valley, the TV towers on South Mountain beat a tempo in red lights. Airplanes, two abreast, floated into Sky Harbor at a regular tempo. The BMW's engine idled gently. I turned and cupped Lindsey's face in my hands, caressing her cheek, the slope of her neck. She turned her lips up to meet my kiss. I ran a hand across her knee, around the edge of her holster, up the silky tension of her stockings, into the taut, loamy warmth of her inner thigh. She sighed happily.

"That," I said, coming up for air, "is the first kiss I ever had on Camelback Mountain. Thanks for fulfilling a fantasy."

"Take me home, Dave, and we'll take care of more fantasies," she whispered.

I slipped the BMW into drive and started down the mountain. It was at the curve into Arcadia Drive that I noticed the white Ford Crown Victoria sitting beside the road with two figures inside. A block farther on, I saw headlights behind us.

Chapter Fourteen

Lindsey left me at the door to my office at the old courthouse. She managed a great kiss despite having a laptop slung over one shoulder and a bag of files over the other. "Anything you want from central records?" she asked. As a matter of fact, there was.

Ten minutes later, I went over to the sheriff's headquarters building on Madison Street myself. It was Friday, five days since Peralta was shot, and I was damned if I was going to hide. My office was claustrophobic. Sheriff Hayden's stern face on the wall demanded answers I didn't have. It felt good to walk, to be out in the warm morning air. The most dangerous thing I encountered was the traffic trying to cross Jefferson Street.

I signed in at headquarters and avoided a covey of civilian employees trying to direct me to meetings. That wasn't why I was there. Three days before, I had ordered Peralta's office locked. I didn't know why Jack Abernathy had been in there the day of the shooting, but I did know I wanted Peralta's aerie off limits to even the senior commanders. Now I used Peralta's keys—Sharon had given them to me yesterday—and let myself in.

His Daytimer sat undisturbed on the credenza: "Mapstone—Camelback Falls." I sat in his big chair, feeling the indentations his body made in the leather through years of staff meetings, phone calls, report reading and late-night brooding. He had settled into that chair the day three years before when I had just returned to Phoenix and accepted his invitation to come downtown to visit. My old partner in the Chief Deputy's office. The world had turned around quite a few times. As I talked about my life, he sat in this chair, swinging back and forth or shaking his leg nervously. He had always been that way. Antsy. Uncomfortable in an office.

But I realized by contrast how much he had changed since I had left the department in 1980. It was something that hadn't been fully disclosed by exchanges of Christmas cards and brief visits every year or two. He seemed to have conquered the moody anger that hid just below his preference for silence. I noticed him bark at a young deputy, but send the man away with a smile and a back pat—definitely a skill the old Peralta didn't have. He had acquired polish and connections, whether from Sharon's rising affluence or a closer relationship with his father or his own grit. He greeted me in a suit and seemed comfortable in it. He took me to lunch at the Arizona Club. Back at his office, I noticed a photo on the wall of him laughing with an elderly Barry Goldwater.

When I ran out of words that day, he merely reached into a drawer, produced a thick file folder, and tossed it to me. "Look into that, will you?" he said. "I just want to know what you think." It was a forty-year-old murder case, unsolved. I don't know if he really expected anything from me. But he had the instincts of a proud man, and he gave his gifts accordingly. At the end he needled me. "Mapstone, I hope all those years chasing young skirts on campus didn't fry your brains."

Now I thought, You would know about that, my friend, wouldn't you?

I shut out my interior voices of doubt and caution, and began a gentle inventory of the room. The bathroom was spotless and empty, save for a can of cheap shaving cream, a safety razor, and a uniform hanging in its cleaning bag. A closet held file cabinets and a safe. But the file cabinets were stuffed with personnel records—I resisted the temptation to check mine—and the safe was empty, its door open. Over at the conference table, I found a well-worn county budget, along with architectural renderings and blueprints for the new Fourth Avenue Jail. They were probably just as he had left them Monday before going to the swearing-in. I lifted seat cushions, looked behind the furled Arizona flag. Various law enforcement magazines sat on a coffee table in front of the leather sofa.

I returned to his desk, sank into the big chair again. Swiveling it, I attacked the credenza, with its geologic strata of files and reports. I didn't have time to inventory every file, but the labels didn't draw my attention. Murder, mayhem, and memos. Then I turned to the desk drawers. A Smith & Wesson 9mm pistol sat in the top drawer, barrel facing toward the front of the desk. I popped out the magazine—loaded, all right. I replaced it and moved on.

The bottom drawer was locked. I worked my way through his heavy key ring until one key fit. Inside the drawer were ammunition, mace, handcuffs, cigars, and a file folder. A bolt shot up my spine when I saw the hand-written label: "Leo O'Keefe."

I set it aside and walked in a wide circle, adding more wear to the institutional carpet. I leaned into the narrow window and stared down to the street. If I went further, I might be interfering with the integrity of the Internal Affairs investigation. Outside, a little boy and an elderly woman were crossing at the light. I thought of me and Grandmother. I didn't know why that made sad down to my bones. Why did Peralta have a file on Leo O'Keefe? Why had I come here today? The neat historical analogies that would give me some confidence stayed frozen in my head.

I went back to the desk and opened the file.

I'd seen some of this before, the reports on the Guadalupe shooting, the plea bargain with O'Keefe. But some was new. Peralta had highlighted a memo from the county attorney noting that O'Keefe should get prison time because he had been arrested at the scene of the shooting armed with a .38-caliber pistol. That was all wrong. I had searched him myself, and there was no gun. Indeed, the next sheet of paper was the evidence log from Guadalupe, with no mention of a pistol in O'Keefe's possession.

On this sheet, Peralta had highlighted all of the items logged in from O'Keefe: cigarettes, wallet, $4.32 in cash. No gun. I had never seen the memo on the gun before.

The file also held a patrol car inventory log. It was routine for deputies to check out the equipment in a car when coming on duty each shift. They noted all this in a log that was filed with the shift supervisor. This one was for unit 4-L-20, dated May 31, 1979, and signed "V. Bullock." Otherwise, it looked unremarkable. At the start of their ill-fated shift, Bullock and Matson found a cruiser with a full tank of gas, engine fluids OK, siren and lights OK. The trunk held flares, traffic cones, and inflated spare tire. The deputies brought their 12-gauge shotgun, report case, and first-aid kit, all duly noted for the sergeant. What could have interested Peralta about this inventory after all these years?

Beneath that was the beat sheet from May 31, 1979. I hadn't seen one of these in years: the assignments, car by car, beat by beat. The 3 P.M. to 11 P.M. shift was commanded by Sergeant Peralta. The watch commander for the station in Mesa was listed as "J.B. Abernathy." I shook my head hard, trying to restore memory. I had forgotten that Abernathy, then a lieutenant, was filling in that month in the East County.

Peralta also had a copy of the radio log from that awful day. With a yellow magic marker he had noted every movement called in by Matson and Bullock. But not the traffic stop that caused their deaths—they never notified the dispatcher they were out with a stopped vehicle. That was against the rules—any stop was supposed to be called in—and it was the cause of our desperate uncertainty that night about who needed assistance. In the wake of the deputies' murders, that breach had been forgotten. Still, it seemed to be what had attracted Peralta's attention. Why hadn't they called in the traffic stop? Were they stubborn old veterans flouting the rules, or was it something else?

Then a letter on departmental stationary, dated May 6, 1979: "Re: Reserve Deputy Harold Matson." It looked like something out of a personnel file. Some brass hat on Madison Street was upset that the Sheriff's Office was getting dunned by Matson's creditors. Most reserve deputies had day jobs or owned businesses. The reserves were a cheap way for the SO to augment its forces and reward political friends of the sheriff. I gathered from the letter Matson had some kind of towing business that had gone sour, and now the lenders were in full cry. It put Matson on thirty days' probation.

The letter was getting brittle. It resisted turning. And behind it was a note. On it, in Peralta's handwriting: "Jonathan Ledger— Camelback Falls."

I let out a long breath. For the first time, Camelback Falls was linked to the Guadalupe shooting. But how?

I was jolted by the soft trill of the telephone. Who in the state of Arizona could think Peralta would be here to answer his telephone? But suddenly the room felt close and breathless. The phone kept trilling. I checked the digital readout: an extension in the building.

I picked it up. "Yeah."

"What's taking you so long? Did you find it?" a man's voice came back. I felt a second of disorientation and exposure. But I pulled my wits back together.

"Yeah," I said. "Where should I meet you?"

There was the briefest pause on the other end of the line. Then, "Who the hell is this? Who is this?"

"This is Sheriff Mapstone. Who are you?"

He hung up before. I got the last sentence out.

I dialed the operator, asked about the extension. "It's an unassigned number in the custody bureau," she said. "Do you want me to ring that number?"

I said no. It was time to go. Past time to go. I closed the file folder, thought about taking it with me. But I locked it back up in the desk drawer. The rear hallway was deserted as I stepped out and secured the door to Peralta's office.

In the lobby, I ran into Lindsey. "What are you doing here?" she asked.

"I figured I'd be safe in a police station." I smiled. "Did you find what I needed?"

She nodded. "No Social Security number, no date of birth, but that doesn't stop your intrepid cyber-searcher."

As we walked out into the midmorning sun, Lindsey handed me the address of Lisa Cardiff.

Chapter Fifteen

Outside, we had barely crossed the arid plaza of the county courts building when we were intercepted by Jack Abernathy.

"Give us a minute, Deputy," he said to Lindsey. The way he said "deputy" made me think he really wanted to say "missy" or "girl," but maybe I was judging the man harshly based on surface impressions. That had gotten me in trouble before.

But there it was. Abernathy, a high-ranking law enforcement official in the nation's sixth-largest city, looked like a Southern sheriff who had stepped out of a sequel to *Smokey and the Bandit*. At best, he was an ancestor mask in the tribe of the police.

In a way, I felt sorry for him. He must have been an embarrassment to the former sheriff, who turned the department into a trendy place of mission statements, media events, and master's-degreed deputies. And he sure didn't fit Peralta's mold. But somehow he hung on. Abernathy was a head shorter than I was. His jowly face was a patchwork of reddened skin, as if he constantly scratched himself. His hair was close-cropped like a dry lawn and going white. All his weight congealed into his belly, which stretched impatiently against the fabric of his uniform shirt. And that Texas in his accent. I half expected him to address me as "boy."

"Sheriff, we got a problem at the jail." He nodded toward the massive brown fortress of the Madison Street Jail complex. I waited and he went on. One inmate had attacked another last night, nearly cutting his head off with a homemade knife.

Both were leaders in respective African American and Latino ("Mescan" in Abernathy's butchered language) gangs. Everyone expected reprisals and tensions were high.

"What do you think we should do?" I asked. He pulled his chin back into his heavy neck, seeming surprised someone, even the greenhorn acting sheriff, had asked his opinion.

"Move some of 'em out," he said. "Disperse 'em to other facilities."

"Well, let's do that, and find out how this moron got a knife into our main jail."

Abernathy pursed his lips and nodded. It went on a long time. A cool breeze was blowing down Jefferson Street from the west. Maybe it would push some of the smog away. Over Abernathy's shoulder, I watched workers finishing the new Federal Building. It was a massive glass objet d'art. I guess the famous architect intended it to convey openness in a democratic society, rather than the respect and awe inspired by government buildings even into the 1930s. But to me it just looked insignificant and ugly, like a credit-card call center in the suburbs.

Finally, Abernathy said, "How are you feeling after that dude took a shot at you?" It came out harsh and confrontational. I said I was OK.

"I can't believe Phoenix PD and Davidson's people, and all Kimbrough's detectives, can't find this little scumbag," he said. I didn't want to take the time to explain, again, why I didn't think Leo O'Keefe had shot at me.

"How is Chief Peralta?" he demanded.

"The sheriff is the same," I said. "In a coma."

"I ought to go by," he said, thrusting his hands into his pants pockets. "You know, he and I go way back."

I let that one sit on the concrete between us. Lindsey was across the street smelling flowers by the old municipal building. She gave me a little wave.

"This logbook from Nixon," he said. "This is not good."

I felt the balls of my feet tense. "That's confidential information, Jack."

"Word gets around the department," he said, working his jaw like he was chewing tobacco. "You know, Dean Nixon was trouble. Long time before we finally got him out. You check his file. I know he was a friend of yours."

"I don't know if he was a friend...," I stammered. "We knew each other in high school."

"He recommended you," Abernathy said. "I sat on your review board for the academy, remember?"

Actually, I didn't remember.

"I voted against you," Abernathy said, not unkindly. "I thought you were some egghead who would get bored with law enforcement. Those kind of people don't like rules, don't like routines. They're a pain in the ass for the supervisors..."

"They probably can even read the little card that has the Miranda warning."

He laughed once, high and breathy and alien. "You're a clever one."

"Well," I said, "Lucky for you I don't hold a grudge."

"Nixon would go crazy, you know." Abernathy didn't meet my eyes. He stared over my shoulder, at the early lunch congregants at Patriot's Park. "One time I saw him nearly beat a suspect to death. Would have, if I hadn't stopped him. He was drinking all the time. Probably taking drugs, too. Then he fell in with those bounty hunters..."

"Jack, what do you think this logbook means?"

He kept his gaze over my shoulder. "How the hell would I know that?"

"You brought it up, Jack."

"Shit." His face reddened, evening out the patches of red and white. "I don't have a clue what it means. I don't know what you're getting at." He fixed me with his little eyes. They were liquid gray. "Don't you know what this kind of thing can do to this department? Look what's happened over in L.A. with the Rampart scandal. Months and months of allegations, careers ruined. Politicians make hay over this. And in the end nothin' changes. I tell you one thing, the only people it helps is the politicians and the bad guys."

I started to speak but he cut me off. "You ain't never gonna get cops to roll over on each other." His voice had changed. Never polished, it had dropped into a rougher clone of itself. I could almost imagine him interrogating a suspect back when he was on the streets. "There's a code of silence, Professor. You think anybody's going to talk about this log, even if it's true?"

I said, "I guess if we have badge numbers, that might lubricate some memories." He worked his heavy jaw again. Maybe he didn't know that detail. I went on. "This isn't some petty-ass IA investigation, like over in Mesa where the male and female officers were taking breaks on duty to go off and fuck. We're talking about murder and attempted murder."

"You don't know that," he squealed. A pair of young women walking by stared at us. "You got your suspect in both shootings. This O'Keefe character. And, hell, with Dick Nixon, nothin' he was involved in would surprise me." I hadn't heard someone use his nickname in years. "Bad things have a way of comin' back around."

"What were the River Hogs, Jack?"

"Bunch of idiots drinkin'," he said, no hesitation. "When they'd get off duty, they'd drive down into some deserted spot in the riverbed, drink and party all night."

"Did you ever go with them?"

His mouth puckered and he shook his head. "I know you're tryin' to get the old white guy. I'm not 'with it' in this department. I don't read the same books as you. I'm not politically correct. But I'm sure as hell not a dirty cop."

"I didn't say you were."

"I supported you for acting sheriff."

Thanks, I guess, I thought.

Suddenly, he calmed down. "OK, Sheriff," he said. "I'll get moving on those prisoner transfers. That oughta help. We wouldn't want a jail riot your first week in office." He added,

"You looked good on television Wednesday. We need somebody like you, clever."

He clapped me on the arm and walked away.

"Jack," I called, and he turned to face me, all belly and jowls. "What about it? You ever go out with the River Hogs?"

He just gave me a little smile, raised a fat finger to his lips—shhhhhhh—then turned and walked on.

There was a disturbance off to my left, and my involuntary muscles sent my hand reaching for the Python under my coat. But it was just some domestic thing, woman and man and their lawyers arguing. A pair of burly young deputies intervened. The male deputies like their hair cut close these days. When I was a young deputy, the fashion was just the opposite: The old guys like Abernathy had crew cuts and the young cops tried to get away with hair as long as possible. I had lived long enough to see a cycle.

So I jaywalked and caught up with Lindsey.

"What did he want?" she asked.

"I guess to tell me I'm clever."

Chapter Sixteen

Friday afternoon skulked by, passed in difficult meetings. The most difficult of all I postponed a day. After I left Abernathy, I drove out to the capitol and went into the mud-colored modern tower that looks very much like the Madison Street Jail. Inside, however, are offices for the governor, attorney general, and other high honchos. The thing looms like a bad hangover behind the lovely little capitol building, built in celebration of statehood in 1912 and crowned with a dome of copper.

I was there to meet the attorney general, and she saw me alone in a small conference room lined with new lawbooks and smelling of copy-machine toner. The AG was a popular Democrat in a Republican state, and she listened intently as I briefed her on the Nixon logbook. She wanted to have her office enter the investigation at once, of course. I should have expected that. These were dirty cops, not some garden-variety Arizona real estate scam. And if my theory was true, they were dirty cops who had murdered Dean Nixon and attempted to murder Peralta. I was more surprised by my reaction: defensive, testy—as if I'd been a bureaucrat in the Sheriff's Office for years, as if I were Abernathy.

If I were still in the history business, I could write a grand and impenetrable paper on the way organizational cultures write themselves upon the individuals in charge. But I've always been a believer in individuals as movers of history, something that got me into trouble with the gasbags of conventional wisdom at the faculty club. No, I was protecting Peralta, plain and simple. That's why I wanted to keep this mess in the Sheriff's Office until we were sure what it was. But I was running out of time—she agreed to give me a week before her investigators intervened.

My meetings with the county attorney, county commissioners, and Chief Wilson of the Phoenix Police were just as stressful. I'm sure they were full of nuance and comedy. But I wasn't really paying attention. I was going through the motions, carrying information. And I was still trying to understand what the discoveries of the past few days really meant. How the hell had Abernathy learned about the logbook? Why was Peralta so concerned with reports from the Guadalupe shooting? What did O'Keefe mean when he said Peralta was shot because "they can't let any of this come out"? Was that why Nixon was murdered, too, and why someone took a crack at me? Who were "they"?

A week ago, I occupied a sweet little sinecure. Now, what a mess.

The western sky was putting on its nightly show—tonight narrow bands of clouds were inventing new colors, somewhere on the spectrum between purple and pink—as we crossed through the saguaro-spiked arroyos and hills of Dreamy Draw and dropped down into the Paradise Valley section of Phoenix. This had been desert when I was a kid. Now, the white lights of suburban safety stretched north and east for miles until they jammed up and faded into the base of the McDowell Mountains. At the Cactus Road exit, I wheeled the car off the freeway, then passed a couple of miles of identical strip shopping centers until Lindsey spotted the sports bar. Inside, just as she had promised, was a woman wearing a blowsy long dress and a red sweater with a needlepoint cat design.

Life is complicated, as Sharon said. Lisa Cardiff—it was Lisa Cardiff Sommers now—had readily agreed to meet us anywhere but her home. I would have preferred a place like Tarbell's down on Camelback Road, or even Tom's Tavern downtown. But it quickly became clear that Lisa, like many north Phoenicians, rarely came down into the "old" part of the city. Anyway, we were on duty and, with my new job, I had a damned example to set. Now, at the entrance to the sports bar and dressed to blend in with chinos and sweatshirts, we greeted her and discreetly showed our IDs, which she studied at some length. After we were shown to a table, we absurdly ordered coffees and Diet Cokes while *SportsCenter* blared on half a dozen TVs.

Franklin Roosevelt had a mistress, despite his heavy leg braces and a world war to run. So did LBJ, and Kennedy and Clinton had racked up impressive body counts. Before us, if Sharon was to be believed, was a woman who had been involved with Peralta. It was a side of him that had utterly hidden itself from me for a quarter century.

Lisa Cardiff Sommers hardly looked like a saucy home-wrecker. But the journey from nineteen years old to the edge of forty was unpredictable. Lisa was shorter than Lindsey, and comfortably filled out, though not fat. She wore flat shoes with ill-fitting footlets. Her brown hair was short. Her face, tanned and pleasant in an unremarkable way, looked like it was comfortable smiling and laughing. Which she wasn't doing now.

"I hope you understand how impossible this is for me," she started out. "Whatever happened when I was a kid is so far in the past. I'm married and have two children, and there's no way I should even be talking to you."

My Diet Coke was flat and I was bone-tired. I said, "Do you understand Sheriff Peralta is in a coma and his assailant is loose? We don't have time to ass around. We could have just shown up at your front door."

"Screw you," she said with vehemence, her lips suddenly draining of any color. "I don't even have to talk to you!"

She started to rise, but Lindsey lightly touched her hand. "Please, Lisa, we need your help."

Maybe it was classic good cop, bad cop, or maybe it was the way Lindsey could disarm and soothe people. Lisa Cardiff

Sommers sat back down and took a long swig of coffee. I could have calmed her down with a martini at Tarbell's.

She said, "Deputy, I can't imagine anything I could tell you—"

"Call me Lindsey."

"That's my daughter's name!" She softened, melted. I felt like such a heel. Lisa said, "It's spelled L-y-n-n-s-y."

"That's nice," Lindsey said warmly, although I knew she would hate the spelling.

Lisa ignored me and went on. "Lynnsy just turned six, and her brother Chance is eight. Do you have children, Lindsey? No? Oh, but I see you're engaged." Lindsey gave her a warm, single-family-detached-home smile. Lisa looked back at me and said, in a tone of motherly correction, "I hope she picked someone more sensitive and empathetic than you."

"He's a great guy," I said. "I hate him."

Lindsey tried to steer Lisa back on course, but she just started crying and talking, like some cheaply constructed dam had given way under pressure of a sudden storm.

"I love my husband and he's a good man. Jim's the southwest regional sales manager for Qwest Wireless. We have a good life. He's a wonderful provider. But Jim couldn't handle knowing about this. He just couldn't. And I'm entitled to my privacy." She sipped coffee and wiped her eyes with a paper napkin.

My God, I thought, she must think we're here on some morals charge. But nobody thinks straight when the subject of old lovers comes up.

"I was nineteen years old when we became involved," she said, a croupy whisper. "I was a kid, for God's sake. I was just having fun. Didn't you do things like that, Lindsey?"

"Sure," Lindsey said. "It's OK." She held Lisa's hand.

"How do you think it's been since he became chief deputy and such a celebrity...," She never said the words "Mike Peralta," as if they had dangerous conjuring power. "People don't usually get to be reminded on TV and in the newspapers about their youthful indiscretions. And that wife of his, on the radio!" She sniffled again. "Of course, I was sick when I heard he had been shot." She looked at me, and drew herself up straighter. "But I just feel so dirty and violated that you've come here. I had to lie to my husband, tell him I had a girlfriend that was having trouble."

Lindsey said, "Lisa, we're not here to invade your privacy. We really just need your help remembering. It may be that some things going on in Sheriff Peralta's life twenty years ago have something to do with the shooting."

Lisa's face softened again and she blew her nose loudly. She had green eyes that seemed speckled with other colors.

"Of course, I'll try to help," she said.

Lindsey tiptoed in. "Did Peralta ever seem like he was having trouble, back when you knew him? Anything at all?"

Lisa stared into the half-empty coffee cup. She gave a little smile. "He was very driven, very intense. I really got that danger charge out of being with him." In a different voice, she said, "He wasn't happy in his marriage. But what happened between us wasn't his fault. I met him when he came to my apartment after there had been a break-in. Later, I found a reason to see him again. He was very shy and awkward, but in this very wonderful adult way. I picked him up. Threw myself at him, is more like it."

I felt a queasy voyeuristic thrill, like listening to people make love loudly in the next room. I drank the flat Coke as penance.

"When did you guys break up?" Lindsey asked.

"January of 1979," she said. "It was on a Sunday night. He said he had to stop seeing me. His wife..."

"And you didn't see him again?"

"Once, years later, I saw him at a distance in Fry's one night. I didn't try to say hello."

That ruled her out of any direct memory of Peralta after the Guadalupe shooting.

"What else was going on in his life?" Lindsey prodded. "Did he ever talk about work?"

"He had..." Lisa laughed out loud. "He had this partner who was, like, trying to become a college professor. He sounded

pretty full of himself, this partner, with his big words and books.
I don't remember his name." Lindsey kicked me under the table.
Lisa said, "Mike was very down-to-earth." She spoke the name
tenderly.

"Now that I look back, it was a weird time," she continued.
"I was born in 1959, so I was too young to be with the real
boomers. They had the sixties. Mike served in Vietnam. My
sister, she got maced by the Chicago police at the Democratic
Convention, and she lived in a commune for awhile. She was
at Altamonte when the Rolling Stones played and there was the
big riot. Kids her age had such a bond, I guess. My age, we got,
like, the BeeGees…"

"Did you meet any people Peralta worked with?" Lindsey
asked.

She shook her head. "We had lots of cops come to the coffee
shop where I worked, but usually not deputies. I worked in
Scottsdale. It was kind of cool, because he was my secret." She
suddenly sounded nineteen again.

Lindsey said, "Please don't be angry if I ask this, but I assume
you guys exchanged gifts?"

"He never gave me diamonds and pearls, if that's what you
mean."

I felt the muscles in my back relax a bit.

"He gave me a mermaid, a little china thing you could have
picked up at Los Arcos mall for ten dollars. I was going through
a mermaid phase. I thought it was sweet of him."

"Did he have any other friends?" I ventured softly. "Other
than this stuffed-shirt partner?"

She thought about it and cocked her head in a wry smile.
"I do remember one," she said. "Because he had such a name.
Nixon, like the president."

"Did you ever meet him?"

"No," she shook her head. "He told me Nixon was a crazy
dude, and I needed to stay away from cops anyway. I always
wanted to meet his friends, to have him take me out with the
boys, show me off, maybe. I was very fearless and stupid. But it

sounded like they'd have fun. Get off duty and go down to the riverbed with a keg of beer. It wasn't like there was a lot to do in Phoenix back then. They even had this cute name for their parties. The River Hogs."

Chapter Seventeen

Driving home, Lindsey and I had a short, sharp fight about the '70s. I found myself in that worst of debating positions, defending an argument I didn't really believe. Resolved: The decade of the 1970s was a pretty good time, after all.

"How can you be saying that?" Lindsey shot back, and not quietly. "Are you envious of Peralta for having a chick on the side?"

"Of course not," I said. "That's not what we're talking about. Infidelity has occurred in every decade." Ah, the debater's half-Nelson. It only made things worse.

"That doesn't make it right," she said firmly. Then, "Dave, you're making me sound like some kind of prude. That's not fair."

"I just get tired of the X-ers blaming everything on the Boomers," I said. "And ten years of complicated events and social forces can't be reduced to one or two clichés."

"I didn't say that," she said. Like all fights between people who love each other, this one was full of ciphers and code strings, and not at all about what it appeared to be. In a softer voice, she added, "You know, I had to raise myself because of all those good times and complicated social forces."

"I know." It was all I could say. She spoke the truth. "I didn't have much fun back then myself," I said. "I could barely get a date. The young women didn't seem interested in me. I never had the great lines that the personality boys have."

"Oh, you're a personality boy, Dave," Lindsey said. Out of my peripheral vision, I could see her luminous smile. "A thinking woman's personality boy." She put her hand on my neck and rubbed—oh, that felt good!

"Now you're flattering me. Don't stop rubbing."

"And," she said, "true personality boys don't have lines. They have stories."

"That unmarked car is still behind us," I said, as we exited to the Seventh Street ramp and paused at the light. Two homeless men, with clothes, beards, and skin the same color as a paper bag, stared at us from behind hand-lettered cardboard signs. Several car lengths back, the Ford had also taken the exit and now prepared to shepherd us home.

"Kimbrough is nothing if not efficient," Lindsey said. "I guess they don't trust me to be your bodyguard."

"Should we stop at Good Sam?"

She stroked my arm. "You know they won't let us up at this hour, Dave."

"He's the only one with the answers."

"I know," she said, as the light turned green and the traffic surged onto Seventh. "I've started a database for you."

"You are so good to me."

"Seriously, personality boy." She poked me gently in the ribs. "I took a month out of Nixon's logbook, May 1979, when the Guadalupe shooting happened. I also scanned in the duty rosters and beat lists for the East County patrol district for the same time period."

"So that we can see if any interesting patterns emerge when we compare everything?" I said.

"Exactly. That may give you a few more answers, at least."

The stucco houses on Cypress Street gave off a happy, Friday night glow. I drove around the block once, just to make sure everything looked right at home. It did, and I was really ready for a drink, a book, Duke Ellington on the stereo, and a warm bed with my woman, who is definitely no prude.

<><><>

Kimbrough brought bagels and bad news to the doorstep next morning. We all migrated into the kitchen, which was bathed in sun before noon, where I fixed coffee for Kimbrough and Lindsey.

"The Justice Department is on our backs," he said, settling into one of the white straight-backed chairs at the kitchen table, and setting a file folder before him like a place mat. It was Saturday, but he was wearing a blue blazer, and a subdued burgundy tie with a crisp white shirt.

"About?"

"The logbook."

"So they won't even give us time to complete our own Internal Affairs investigation?"

"I'm just telling you what I heard from a friend at the U.S. Attorney's Office."

I opened up the *Republic*, half expecting to see giant headlines about a scandal in the Sheriff's Office. But the front page was full of idiot consumer news. Plus a prominent smog story. The Phoenix Open promoters must be getting worried.

"It's obvious to me," I said, "that Peralta was already looking into the Guadalupe shooting and whatever Nixon was involved with." I told Kimbrough about Camelback Falls, the file in Peralta's desk drawer, and the conversation with Lisa Cardiff Sommers.

"Jesus," he said. "You're supposed to be holding together a department that's about to come apart. Instead, you're running your own little private investigation here."

Irritation was wired all through his body language. I poured coffee, trying not to let a defensive little tremor show in my hand.

"I had some hunches, that's all."

"Well, let me give you another interpretation," he said. "Peralta's dirty."

"What?" Lindsey jerked her shoulders back.

Kimbrough knotted his brow and plowed ahead. "I know the man is lying in a coma, and I care about him, too. But I can't just wish away his badge number in that log book, entered next to sizable amounts of money. And we're running out of time."

He sampled the coffee, then sipped deeper. "Maybe Nixon was blackmailing Peralta? Maybe Nixon raised the stakes too high and Peralta killed him, I got the lab work back yesterday, and Nixon was dead at least twelve hours before Peralta was shot."

I felt blood rushing into my face. "This is nuts."

"David, we found one of Peralta's new business cards there in Nixon's trailer. One of the cards with him as sheriff, not chief deputy. I checked and those were only delivered two weeks ago. So within the past two weeks, Peralta and Nixon have had contact."

"Well, if Peralta was going to kill Nixon, would he leave a damned business card?"

"Maybe it didn't start out that way," Kimbrough said. "Maybe they had an initial meeting and just talked. Something went wrong. Nixon tried to put the squeeze on Peralta, whatever." Kimbrough made a gun barrel out of his finger. "Bam, end of problem. But maybe he's interrupted before he can clean up the evidence."

"It sounds to me like Peralta was investigating this case himself!" I heard my voice echo angrily off the wall.

"Hear me out, if you're going to play Lone Ranger," Kimbrough said through gritted teeth. "Think of the pressure Peralta could have been under. He's about to be sworn in as sheriff, and here's this scumbag Nixon blackmailing him."

Lindsey said, "So then Peralta finds a way to shoot himself on the day of his swearing in? Just to make it look good?"

"No." Kimbrough's eyes were large and earnest, incapable of irony. "There was obviously some kind of double-cross. Maybe Peralta had threatened to implicate the other dirty cops, those other badge numbers. And one of them had to take him out. David, I have seen the list of badge numbers in the logbook. There are nine current Sheriff's Office employees among them. Nine. Including Peralta. There are fourteen former deputies, including Matson and Bullock."

"Damn it," I said, "none of this is proven yet. I didn't even want to know that information before Internal Affairs completes its investigation. These deputies deserve due process."

"The point is," Kimbrough said, "who knows what kind of shit these cops were into twenty years ago? Maybe they were still in it this year. Those kind of people would go to any lengths to keep it covered up."

I poured myself some orange juice and put some salmon spread on a bagel. My stomach hurt.

"There's just one problem," I said. "Yesterday's prime suspect, Leo O'Keefe."

"He's probably involved somehow," Kimbrough said. "Maybe O'Keefe is the tie-in at this Camelback Falls thing. But in the real world, we have to go for the quickest path that's going to break a case. Who has the bigger motive for murder here, some convict or some dirty cops who could lose everything if their past comes out?"

My anger boiled back up again. "One of them shot at me. So I am presumed dirty, too? How the hell did they even know I was going out at three in the morning to meet O'Keefe?"

Kimbrough said, "You do keep public company with Bobby Hamid."

"Oh, Jesus!"

"Didn't you have dinner at Durant's with Hamid?"

I held out my hands. "Put the cuffs on me. You got me, copper."

Kimbrough slapped the tabletop. "Damn it, Sheriff. How do you explain Peralta's badge number in that book?"

"I can't," I shouted. "Yet. How can you believe this man, who we have both worked with for years, is dirty? Not only that, but that he is in so deep that he's willing to order a murder? Then the other dirty cops could shoot him in retaliation?"

Kimbrough silently studied the table. "I don't know what I believe," he said. "I'm just telling you what the feds are talking themselves into."

"You sounded like a believer."

"I don't know who to trust," he said. "The whole department is just crazy with talk and paranoia about this logbook. You saw it yourself with Abernathy. How the hell did he find out? None of it makes any damned sense. I wish O'Keefe would contact you again."

"That's not likely with your guys always on my tail," I said.

"What?"

Lindsey said, "White Crown Vic. It's been tailing us for a couple of days. We assumed it was you or Phoenix PD."

Kimbrough fell suddenly silent, studying his hands. "David," he finally said. "We haven't had any units following you. The most we've done is ask for extra PD patrols past the house here. Phoenix detectives don't even have Crown Vics now. They make 'em drive Chevy Cavaliers." He sighed. "Jesus Christ, what is going on?" He didn't wait for an answer. "The next damned time you see that car, I want you to call backup. It may be the feds, or it may be connected to whoever took a shot at you the other night. Call for help."

I nodded and tried to eat. The bagel was warm and flavorful, but my insides felt cold and vulnerable. I instinctively stepped away from the kitchen window.

"Shit," Lindsey said. "If it's not the good guys following us…"

"There's something else," Kimbrough said, tapping the folder he had placed on the kitchen table. He traced invisible horizontal lines on the top of the folder. "Look, it takes a lot to make me blush, get it? But we found this stuff with all the trash and wine bottles inside Nixon's trailer. It's pretty heavy duty."

I took the orange juice and pulled up a chair. Kimbrough pushed the folder at me. "I figured since you knew Nixon way back when, maybe this might mean something."

I opened the cover and a half dozen color photos were inside, eight-and-a-half by eleven, lots of skin. Kimbrough was right. The images were extremely explicit. Full frontal nudity and penetration were just the beginning. Check your imaginations at the door for all will be revealed.

"Tryouts for the gymnastics team?" Lindsey said, looking over my shoulder.

It was an orgy. The top photo showed several couples in various copulatory positions. I hadn't been a porn aficionado since we had the secret stack of *Penthouse* at the substation when I was a twenty-year-old deputy. Spectator sports were not my thing. But these photos stood out as, well, real. They had none of the retouched bodies and professional lighting of sex industry images. The people looked average, the moments carried the edge and flaws of the spontaneous.

The scene wasn't some sleazy motel room with a pizza-colored bedspread and velvet Elvis on the walls, either. Take out the writhing bodies and the room could have been in *Architectural Digest*. White marble stairs and levels flowed out of a roomy conversation pit, which contained expensive-looking sectional sofas and spare, modern tables. African sculptures, with stone erections to match the flesh ones of the orgy, stood on one set of shelves. A large abstract painting, hot colors and geometry, dominated one wall, and another wall was all glass. The real eye-catcher, though, was what looked like an indoor waterfall, cascading down from a second level into a pond in the center of the room. But this, too, was not quite a "done" room—you could see the reefers, pills, and cocaine scattered around various tables.

The second photo stopped me. It centered on a man with Mark Spitz hair, naked except for dirty white socks. He was upright, on his knees, connected doggy-style to a curvy brunette who had matted hair and wore a black merry widow. Her face was buried in a cushion. The man had turned his head to face the cameraman, giving a goofy-drunk grin and looking so young I didn't recognize him at first.

"That's Nixon," I said.

"Holy shit," Kimbrough said. "So much for stereotypes about the relative physical endowments of white men."

"That's how he got his nickname," I said. "He was very popular with women."

"Oh, please," Lindsey said. "Men with giant cocks are bad lovers. They think they don't have to do anything else but show up."

How did she know that? A tremor of insecurity swept through me. But turning back to the picture, I felt the same dizzy, intrusive feeling as when we talked to Lisa the night before. We weren't meant to see these photos. They were Dean's trophies, from when he was virile and desirable and the world existed in a happy teacup of youth and promise.

I set it face-down. The next photos showed a pretty young girl fellating an older man. He sat Buddha-like on an Eames chair with the girl on her knees. His skin was leathery brown, but he had an old man's spidery stretch lines around his stomach. They were in the same room, but closer to the waterfall, the spray sluicing off white marble behind the two lovers. A display of red, black, and orange pills was splayed across a nearby tabletop. Next to that was a hand mirror with neat lines of what might have been baking soda, but wasn't.

The girl was truly beautiful, with a heart-shaped face, flaxen hair parted in the middle, and an exquisite young body, lightly tanned. She looked languidly at the camera.

Something kicked my memory. I knew her.

"What?" Lindsey said.

"That's Marybeth," I said. "Marybeth Watson. The girl who was with Leo that night in Guadalupe. She was his girlfriend."

"Not when this picture was taken," Lindsey said. "You know who this is with her?"

I studied the man's face. He wasn't looking right at the camera. Something about his wispy white rim of hair contrasted with dramatic black eyebrows looked familiar. But I had to shake my head.

"That," said Lindsey, "is Jonathan Ledger, the author of *The Sex Instructions*."

I sat back in the chair and pointed at the photos. "So this must be Camelback Falls."

Chapter Eighteen

Draw me a map of the human heart. Show me the roads in and out. Where does Eros take the turnoff from love, darkness from passion? Destiny, fate. Nixon, Peralta, and me, we were all just cops together. Men with easily pierced skin and breakable bones. Men with hearts. But all along we were connected by invisible strands that ran to right now: Nixon dead, Peralta in a coma, Mapstone the sheriff. Badge numbers in the logbook. Photographs on my breakfast table.

Draw me a map of the human heart. The back roads of jealousy and rage. It is no coincidence that cops get killed during family fights. At the point of conjugal connection the mask of civilization is always shaky, our mastery of nature most personally at risk. Love and lust are dangerous things, and every civilization tries to control them, whether through ancient commandments or the latest dating code on campus. Nature is always ready to slip the leash, go mad again. We Phoenicians should know this most of all, living in our artificial city with the desert seemingly subdued for our pleasure and recreation. But beneath us are the ruins of the Hohokam city that preceded us. They were men with hearts, too, who dug the canals, unlocked the rich soil, vanished. The desert is really in control, merely biding its time.

These thoughts tried to find purchase inside my head as we drove the speed limit through the pleasant streets of northeast Phoenix two hours later. Lindsey was lost in her own thoughts and we didn't talk much. We were in her Honda Prelude, with its bumper sticker that read, "Keep honking, I'm reloading." But the message was lost on our tail from the previous night— no cars appeared to be following us. I was on an errand I most dreaded.

Judge Carlos Peralta lived in a rambling ranch house off Lafayette Boulevard in the city's Arcadia district. The houses had been built in the 1950s where citrus groves stood. The judge's house was guarded by lush grapefruit and orange trees, oleanders and desert honeysuckle. Down the freshly cut front lawn was a magnificent view of Camelback Mountain. Lindsey parked in the driveway and kept on her seatbelt.

"You're not coming?"

"Dave, this is definitely an interview that should be one-on-one." She patted my hand.

So I walked up a long sidewalk framed by ornamental lights and flowerbeds. The walk was enchanting at night, like the Thanksgiving five years ago when we all came over. The judge had been a widower here for ten years, but he refused Mike and Sharon's yearly suggestions that he move to a condo. He had been the first Mexican-American on the state appeals court, and the first to move to Arcadia. This house also held his memories and his books. I understood that much.

His housekeeper, Mrs. Sanchez, a large woman with happy black eyes, greeted me and showed me into his study. The room was dark in the way that comforts the old or the grieving. It was a vast repository of books: on the walls, on tables, on the desk that looked out-of-place modern, even in stacks on the thick cream carpet. Amid a table full of family photos was a large picture of his son as an Army Ranger. Another showed him as chief deputy, his expression barely changed across three decades. Gas logs glowed in a fireplace. It was about 70 degrees outside, so they had to run the air conditioning to have the illusion of winter inside. And at the far end of the room, swallowed up in a leather armchair, was the frail figure of the judge.

"Come in, David." I could hear his wheezing across the room.

"Please don't stand, sir." I crossed the room quickly and took his hand. I could feel bones barely covered with skin. His expression was concealed in the half shadow. The room smelled of Mentholatum. I felt like a nightstick had repeatedly been jabbed into my abdomen.

"I'm sorry to trouble you, Judge…"

"Why don't you call me Carlos?"

"Carlos," I said. But it was no good. "I can't, Judge. It just goes against my grain. The way I was raised, I suppose."

"Understood," he said. "When I was your age it was inconceivable that I would address an older person by his first name. Now every stranger talks to me like I am four years old."

"We've had a development in the case," I said. He was silent, so I went on, speaking through the acid I could sense creeping up my throat. "A former deputy was found murdered, a man who used to work with me and Mike in the East County." I watched his weathered face, but no expression registered. "We're not sure if he was killed by the same person who shot Mike last Monday. But this man, whose name was Dean Nixon, left some evidence…"

I just let it hang there for a minute as my eyes were drawn into the conjuring flame of the gas fireplace. I looked away, scanned some of his books. There was Eisenhower's *Crusade in Europe*, Octavio Paz's *The Labyrinth of Solitude*, several volumes of Plato and Locke. The judge said nothing.

"The evidence is a logbook that may show payoffs to sheriff's deputies from years ago, from the 1970s."

"Is my son among them?"

The words were spoken with no emotion. I could imagine the cool litigator of a half-century ago. I said, "Yes, he appears to be. But we are very early in the invest—"

"I didn't want him to be a policeman, do you know that?"

I shook my head.

The judge inhaled loudly and said, "From the earliest, I wanted him to be a man of the law, a lawyer. I suppose that guaranteed he would rebel against me."

"I know he always revered you," I blurted.

"We didn't speak for years," the judge said. I didn't know that either, although I had always sensed a distance between father and son, like magnets repelling. He went on. "I was severe. I had worked very hard to make it in the Anglo world, and here was my son making common cause with men who, in my memory, would stop and beat a Mexican-American for sport. I told him, 'You will be nothing but the token beaner, the one they call spic behind your back.' He never listened."

The judge raised himself up. It looked painful. But after all the effort, his body seemed even deeper in the chair. "Don't get me wrong," he went on. "I detest today's Balkanization and victim-mongering. My brother always says he is a Chicano. I am an American, of Mexican descent…" He looked toward a small side table, where his hand found a teacup.

"Your evidence doesn't surprise me," he said, sipping from the cup. "Law enforcement always grows corruption."

I shivered a little in the sudden coolness of the room, amazed at the clinical tone of the man opposite me.

"Judge, I'm not saying he was involved."

"When I was elected to the bench in 1965, Maricopa County Superior Court, it was common to see cops plant evidence that damned a suspect, suppress evidence that might exonerate him."

"Common?" I challenged, losing some of my fear of the man.

He ignored me. "In the 1970s, drugs changed everything. The money just added to the opportunities for corruption. I presided over a dozen trials involving law enforcement that had stolen drugs or fallen in with dealers. And that was nothing compared with what the federal judges heard." He smacked his lips loudly. "I always wondered, if these were the stupid ones getting caught, what must be going on that we never even knew?"

My mouth had turned to a dry riverbed. "Are you telling me you suspect your son was involved in corruption?"

"Who do you think shot my son, Sheriff?" he demanded. He didn't wait for an answer. In a higher, softer voice he said,

"Policemen make a lot of enemies. Good ones and bad ones. Just like lawyers. I know I did. And when all this comes out, they won't hesitate to crucify my son, just like they tried to do me. Whatever the truth."

"What do you think the truth is, Judge?"

His breathing fell back into a wheeze. He said evenly, "Lawyers and history professors, both wordsmiths. Both truth-seekers. When we're young we think truth is something that can be bottled and preserved, like some specimen in biology. Now, they tell us everything is relative, that there is no truth, and that's crazy. What do I think? I think a revolution happened in the 1970s, and if that's where your evidence comes from, then all the rules were off."

"This is your son, Judge! Give me something that can help him."

He didn't speak for a long time, just seemed to shrink more into the big leather chair. I finally rose and prepared to go.

"I knew your grandfather Philip, you know."

"Yes."

"He was a good man," the judge said. "He took patients from the barrio when Anglo Phoenix still treated us like dogs. He respected Mexican Americans, understood the dilemma, assimilation versus identity. He always struck me as the epitome of cultivated manliness."

He sighed. "Cultivated manliness, our age doesn't even know what that means." The fireplace glowed yellow-blue, suddenly orange. I half expected to hear a log fall and crackle, but the room was dark silent. "I see some of him in you. David. So I think the best and only help for my son is you."

I retreated. "Thank you, Judge Peralta."

He said, "Do you have the courage to face the truth you find, David?" But he didn't want an answer. In the dimness, I could see he had picked up a book and started reading, his breathing a steady squeezebox wheeze. I quietly let myself out.

Chapter Nineteen

I had begun to tell Lindsey about my talk with Judge Peralta when the cell phone rang and the communications center sent us twenty miles away to a hostage situation near Queen Creek. A former boyfriend was holed up in a double-wide trailer with a woman and her two children. Did I just imagine that the deputies on the scene looked at me differently, with fear and suspicion in their eyes? Did I count too many TV camera crews for just another crime story in the Valley? Bill Davidson was there, too, with a flak vest and a tall cup of Circle K coffee. But if he knew about Nixon's logbook, he didn't let on. He told me it was good to see the sheriff out with the deputies on a Saturday. For a moment, I felt better.

I was milling around the back of the SWAT command post, trying not to get in the way, when the cell phone rang again with another blast from the past.

"David Mapstone?" It was a man's voice, baritone, brisk and impatient. "This is Hector Gutierrez, with Briscoe, Hayne and Douglas."

"Yes, sir."

"I'm making this call as an officer of the court," the voice wobbled over the wireless stations.

"Why is that, Mr. Gutierrez?"

"You're the acting sheriff," he said. "I don't know anything about you." The verdict was final. "You probably don't realize that I used to be in the public defender's office. Years ago, I defended a man named Leo O'Keefe."

"What about O'Keefe?" I cut him off.

"I saw the news. This is the man you think shot Sheriff Peralta."

"What about O'Keefe?"

"He contacted me this afternoon," Gutierrez said.

"How?"

"In the parking garage at my office," he said. "I stopped in for some files, and he was there. He looked like hell. Of course, I told him I couldn't help him, that as an officer of the court I was required to contact the police."

"Did you offer to help him turn himself in?"

There was a long empty buzz on the phone. Finally, "I don't really do pro bono work now, Mapstone."

I couldn't resist, "Is this the same 'Red Hector' who was fighting for the oppressed?"

"To hell with you, Mapstone. I'm doing you a favor. O'Keefe is on the run. I told him to go to the police. But he's afraid. He's convinced they're out to kill him. He's convinced they did everything they could to get him from the day he was found with two dead deputies and that girl in Guadalupe."

"That true?"

"That was a long time ago," Gutierrez said. "You do what you can when you're defending some guy who has every deck stacked against him."

A blast of radio traffic came through the command post. I stepped outside onto the road, facing an alfalfa field and San Tan Mountain, faded in a yellow haze.

"Did he get a fair trial?"

"In my opinion, no. But with two dead cops, nobody was in a hurry to help this kid. Jesus, even his name, Leo-O. Sounds funny."

"What does that mean? Was the case prosecuted kosher?"

"Hell, I don't know. I did the best I could. See, people get lost in the system. It's like this giant threshing machine, and when it gets hold of you everything just kind of goes along automatically."

"Why can't I find his statement in the case file?" I asked. "Was that entered in the defense?"

"That sounds like a Sheriff's Office screwup. Imagine that." He chuckled humorlessly. "He claimed he was set up. That something was going on between the deputies who got killed, and the two fine, upstanding prison escapees who shot them."

I asked him what was going on.

"It was a long time ago. Some dirty cop thing. It was in his statement." I could almost hear him impatiently looking at his Rolex. "Look, he didn't have any family, didn't have any money. He was a long way from home and he hooked up with some bad people."

"What about Marybeth?"

"Oh, the girl? She had a moneybags daddy in the oil business. He hired a big-time lawyer out of Tulsa. They cut her off from Leo so damned fast. Made it sound like she was a kidnap victim—and let me tell you, she had the devil in her. But Leo was seen as the bad guy."

"Was he the bad guy?"

"How the hell should I know, Mapstone? Do you know how much this conversation would cost if you were one of my clients?"

"Consider this a public service, counselor."

"Yeah, right," he said. "No, I thought the kid was in the wrong place at the wrong time, and everybody abandoned him."

"Including you?"

"Hey, screw you, acting sheriff," he snarled through the digital circuits. "I did my part. This is your problem now."

The hostage-taker came out before the evening news. A crew of deputies dressed like Robocop wrestled him into the dust, and Lindsey and I carried out two scared little kids. The public affairs officer said it would make a great photo-op. I was just trying to be useful on a scene. Or maybe I was trying to get ahead of the news cycle, before the shitstorm hit over the logbook and the badge numbers.

We got back in the Prelude and headed to the Superstition Freeway, then turned west into the pink remains of the sunset, headed downtown. Leo O'Keefe was still out there, alive as of this afternoon and still carrying his secrets. I was at a loss as to how to get to him, if he thought the cops were the bad guys. By the time we reached Good Sam to check on Peralta, the cell phone rang again. The battery was nearly dead, and I half expected it was Gutierrez demanding to know where he could send a $1,000-an-hour bill.

"It's Deputy Stevens in the communications center, Sheriff. Captain Kimbrough left word that he needs to meet you tonight. Do you have something to write with?" Lindsey passed me a notepad. I was amazed she actually had old-fashioned paper in the car. "He needs to see you at the Crown Plaza Hotel downtown at nine P.M. tonight."

"And he wants me to meet him there?" Lindsey's blue eyes followed my writing on the notepad. She raised her eyebrows.

"He said it's important, sir. Said you'd know what it was concerning. He didn't give me any further details. He said to meet him in the parking garage on the fourth floor, by the elevator."

Then the phone died.

We walked across 12th Street to the hospital, me musing about our enslavement to technology, how we couldn't get by without gadgets that a few years ago seemed like frills. Suddenly I felt something rushing toward us. Surprise and panic jolted through me. I pushed Lindsey back toward the curb, reached for the Python. It was a Mercedes-Benz the size of a starship, black with black-tinted windows. One of the windows came down with a soft electronic whisper and Bobby Hamid's handsome face peered out.

"You seem tense, Dr. Mapstone."

I muttered something obscene and took my hand off the revolver. I looked around to see how many county supervisors and investigative reporters were there to witness our exchange. But the street was empty in the crisp air of the gathering January night. Bobby opened the door, slid over. Lindsey and I exchanged glances, then we climbed in. What the hell.

"You looked quite heroic on television," he said, turned out in a three-button black coat, jeans, and gray silk T-shirt. "Saving the children in prime time. I do believe the sheriff's hat is growing on you."

"Come on, Bobby," I said, settling into the soft leather of the seats. "You don't want to be my agent."

He regarded me with his amused, feline eyes. Bach was quietly coming out of the car speakers. "How is your little mystery coming along? The River Hogs and all that nostalgia for the disco era?"

"I'm feeling less nostalgic."

"Oh, come, come," he said. "'Disco Inferno,' 'Love to Love You Baby,' K.C. and the Sunshine Band."

"I was more a Springsteen-Eagles-Linda Ronstadt fan," I said, letting Bobby play his game.

"Yes, Linda. 'Love is a Rose.' You know her brother was the Tucson police chief?" Suddenly his eyes went completely opaque, like the windows of the Benz rolling up. "David, someone wants to kill you."

I sat back in the seat. Bobby had sources in law enforcement, don't ask me where. Somehow he had found out about the shots at Kenilworth School. I said, "It's not clear who those shots were directed at."

He looked at me quizzically. "You are obviously giving me credit for knowing about some recent adventure of yours. I am talking of something different."

"Quit screwing around," Lindsey said, her fair skin flushing with anger. "What are you talking about?"

"What they call 'the word on the street,'" Bobby said, momentarily surprised to have been challenged out of his circuitous conversational ways. "The word on the street is that Sheriff Mapstone is a dead man."

"Why?" Lindsey demanded.

"It seems to be something to do with your River Hogs," he said. "It seems that you are into something very dangerous. A man named Nixon, a former deputy sheriff, was murdered, no? And the shooting of Chief Peralta. My sources tell me this is not the work of this escapee, O'Keefe, as your press conference said. As a good citizen, and a friend, I felt I should pass this information along."

"Jesus H. Christ," Lindsey said. "Good citizen, my ass."

Bobby's perfect posture took subtle offense. "Yes, Miss Lindsey. A good citizen and a friend. This isn't a game. These are killers."

"Who are these people?" I asked. "Cops? Deputies?"

"Contrary to Sheriff Peralta's tiresome obsession, I am not plugged in to the underworld."

"But obviously you hear things."

He faced out, staring at the street, content to let us stew in Bach. I looked at Lindsey. Her hair glowed blackly in the reflection of the streetlights. Her eyes looked tired.

"Professor Mapstone," he said, "What was this affair in Guadalupe, in May 1979?"

I studied his face, suspicion in me like a high fever. "It was a shooting. Two old deputies stopped a car with two prison escapees. They killed the deputies. Peralta showed up and killed the escapees."

"I thought you were there?"

"I was. How do you know that?"

"Everyone seems to know," he said. "That word on the street again. Do you really remember what happened there? Twenty years is a long time."

"I remember it all."

He nodded his head slightly. "What happened after the shooting?"

"It was a cop shooting," I said. "Lots of paperwork, lots of Internal Affairs." I felt like I was stuck in an essay test I hadn't studied for. What the hell was he getting at? I knew if I pushed him too far, I'd end up with nothing.

"Why were those two deputies in Guadalupe?" he asked, his voice soft, contemplative.

"It was a traffic stop gone bad. That was obvious when Peralta and I rolled up."

"Really?" he said. "Obvious. Well, eyewitnesses can be unreliable, can't they? That's why we need historians who can sift the evidence with more detachment. Quite an irony for you, Professor Mapstone."

"Shit," I said. "I give up, Bobby. If this is your help, it's not much."

"You give me too much credit," he said, stroking his fine jawline. "I don't know all the answers. Only some of the questions to ask. That ought to be enough."

Lindsey popped the door handle and stepped out. But Bobby gently took my shoulder. "I know this much: You have the trusting nature of the reflective man, the man who wants to live the life of the mind." He looked hard at me, his eyes empty of humanity. "Your department is not what it seems, Sheriff. Remember the Roman emperors who trusted the Praetorian Guard. Trusting will get you killed."

Chapter Twenty

The Crown Plaza Hotel sat at Adams and Central, a big, tan box with half-moon windows, another homely remnant from Phoenix's 1970s building boom. When the Hotel Adams sat on this block, it was a lovely Spanish Mediterranean landmark where the state legislature met informally in the coffee shop, and its awnings shaded Central Avenue from the summer heat. It was built after the first Hotel Adams burned in 1910, the most famous blaze of frontier Phoenix. When I was a little boy—this was 1964—I sat in a car with Grandmother and watched a bank robber chased down by the cops in the alley right beside the hotel. But by the early 1970s, the old Adams was a fleabag, its rooftop neon sign struggling in red letters to say HOT ADA S. It sounded like a whorehouse. The block had history.

Tonight it was so deserted it was as if everyone in the city had silently evacuated, that only Lindsey and I hadn't gotten the word. Spending time in the hospital only added to the sense of oppressive isolation. The doctors were worried about Peralta's lungs. It didn't take a medical degree to know that being flat on your back with a machine doing your breathing was not exactly the way the human body was built to run. Tests showed the beginning of pneumonia in one lung. We sat with Sharon while three doctors gave her a grim catechism of the limitations they were up against with Peralta in a coma. She didn't cry anymore. Her face had taken on the quality of a latex mask atop dangerous emotions. She didn't need to know what I knew. I didn't even know what I knew, if Bobby Hamid was to be believed.

After the hospital, we drove home, drank martinis with olives, and ate baked potatoes with cheese and salsa while we talked about the day. Lindsey wondered about Peralta and his father, how hard it must have been to measure up to a father of such accomplishment and yet such exacting expectations. I wondered about the Peralta stubbornness and fear of showing emotion, keeping both men apart for years I really wanted to go to bed and have her read to me; then I would read to her. But we locked up the house at 8:45, switched to the BMW—I needed to fill up at the 24-hour gas station down on Roosevelt—and drove slowly back downtown.

We drove around the block taking stock of our paranoia.

"I don't want to be afraid to show my face," I said. "I won't do that."

Lindsey scanned the empty sidewalk on Central. "Dave, somebody tried to kill you the other night. You just heard from Bobby Hamid that your life is in danger. Now we're just going to walk into a creepy parking garage at night? And you haven't been able to reach Kimbrough."

It was true. I had tried Kimbrough's cell phone twice since we left the hospital, just to be sure I got the message right about the meeting. But each time I was routed directly to voice mail.

"But what if he needs us?" I said. "He left the message and said it was important. I think the risk is manageable."

"Manageable," she said, her voice flat, assessing not really resisting.

"It's a big hotel right in the middle of the city, video cameras, guards." The light at Adams was red, so I turned in my seat to face her, took her hand. "Lindsey, if I just hide, the bad guys succeed. I didn't want to take this job, but now I've got to do it. Whatever this thing is—they've tried to kill Peralta and now me—it thrives because nobody wanted to touch it, nobody wanted to go there." She just looked at me, her eyes huge and nearly violet. The light turned and I added, "We can always flag down a couple of Phoenix cops on the bike patrol and ask them to escort us."

She wrinkled her nose. "OK, you win." She patted her back-pack absently. It looked reassuringly bulky.

I rolled slowly around the block. The old art deco Valley Bank tower on Monroe was still vacant, an embarrassing eyesore for the umpteenth downtown revitalization attempt. A street person sat in the shadows of the dingy entrance, his shopping cart overflowing with black plastic bags, and dingy comforters. I thought again about Leo O'Keefe, about what Gutierrez said about being caught in the thresher.

At the parking garage entrance, I took a ticket and watched the yellow arm of the gate pop up obediently. A white-haired man watched us impassively from the parking attendant's booth. The BMW climbed up the ramp into the bowels of the build-ing, the engine noise echoing off the colorless prefab concrete walls. Then we leveled out in the long, low garage. The floor had been restriped so many times it was difficult to find the right way to go up. The ceiling was more concrete—too cramped to even allow a minivan beneath it. The decorative half-moon arches facing outside had long ago been fenced off with what looked like wooden pickets painted brown. And even though the streets were deserted, the garage was full of vehicles, parked tightly together, even bumper-to-bumper.

The sardine feeling let up a bit as we wound up to level four, which looked about half full. I scanned the space for any sign of life. Nothing. I swung around the length of the floor, patrolling slowly past empty cars. Then I pointed the BMW back in the direction of the down ramp, just to be safe.

The brightly lit area by the elevators was empty, too. I held my foot on the brake and rolled down the window, listening. The soft, precise timing of the BMW. A low moaning intake fan somewhere. A siren far away, fading. My mind slipped back to Peralta's office, the man's voice: "Did you find it?" What was "it"? Peralta had been looking at the evidence logged in after the Guadalupe shooting. Bobby Hamid had asked, "What happened after the shooting?" How was Jonathan Ledger, the world-famous sex therapist, involved with the girl who was arrested at that shooting?

"Dave."

A pair of headlights swept across the concrete wall ahead of us, and then the businesslike grillwork of a white car appeared at the head of the ramp. It was a Ford Crown Victoria, like a hundred in the Sheriff's Office or the Phoenix PD, the kind issued to detective captains like Kimbrough. But there was no handsome black man inside. These were two white guys, beefy-looking in the glare of the garage lights. They quickly pulled directly in front of us.

"Dave," Lindsey said.

"Call 9-1-1," I said.

"Trying," she said, the cell phone in her hand.

"I don't want to accidentally shoot some civilian who's just asking for directions," I said. But I pulled the Python out of its holster and slid it into the seat between my legs. I scanned the mirrors. The rest of the garage remained lifeless.

They just sat there, looking us over. Their hands were hidden. I studied them. They looked like cops, maybe. Something in the brow—authority? power?—with eyes accustomed to looking wherever they pleased. Thin lips and heavy jaws, no facial hair. Cheap cop haircuts, one black-haired and the other dishwater blond. But something looked wrong, too. One of them wore a heavy chain under his polo shirt. Old cops—they were my age, at least. Former cops?

The BMW was still in drive and I kept my foot on the brake while I measured the garage like a cat measuring a mouse hole. There was no way to get around them. No way out behind. The up ramp was the down ramp. Maybe Kimbrough would suddenly step out of the elevator. Maybe pigs would fly.

"Shit," Lindsey said, laying aside the phone. "No signal. We're under too much concrete."

I thought, Now what, Mr. Ph.D.? The fumes of the two idling cars made the air heavy with toxins. I said, "We can try to run for the exit stairs. Or we can shoot them."

"I like the second suggestion," Lindsey said, undoing her backpack while staring into the Crown Vic.

"How about the middle path," I said. I reached into my coat and produced my star. I held it out the window and shouted at them. "Step out of your car, slowly."

They grinned like I had just told the funniest joke in history. I put the star away and fingered the grip of the Python. I shouted again, "We're sheriff's deputies. Step out of your vehicle, now. Other officers are on the way."

Instantly they flung the big Ford at us. It slammed hard into the front of the BMW, detonating the airbags. The shock of the collision kicked my heart into my throat, and my vision was nothing but white plastic.

"Lindsey!"

"I'm OK," she yelled, off to my side.

I felt the car being pushed backward. That's when I forced myself to inhale, and I drove the accelerator into the floor. We lurched forward, pushing the Ford now. The smell of burning tires and belts pierced my lungs. Then my sight came back. The dashboard and seat wells were draped in deflated airbags. Our antagonists looked much the same. They had obviously disconnected the airbags in the Ford.

They also had the Interceptor engine package and push bar of cop cars, which was more than a match for my fine German engineering. We suddenly lurched backward again. I poured on the power, to no avail. I was glad I couldn't see the dash, where the tachometer needle would be buried in the red.

"They're going to push us out of here!" Lindsey yelled, and we were moving inexorably toward the rear wall, where the flimsy brown picket fence seemed the only thing that would momentarily arrest our fall onto the street below.

I slammed the stick shift into park, and it bit back hard against my hand. Then the car gave out an awful metal-shearing-off-metal groan. Lindsey pulled the emergency brake. The car jerked sideways and we slammed hard into a concrete pillar.

I could hear the Ford snap into reverse, prepare to back off for another try at us. I didn't wait.

"Go!" I pushed Lindsey out of the passenger door, then I climbed over and followed her, running madly toward a row of cars. I heard the Ford's driver drop it back into drive, then tires screeching under acceleration, a bull from Motown hell running at my wounded matador. There was a second's silence, then a sharp struck note, a cascade of rubber, metal, and composites protesting, a ghastly crash against the far wall. I had just enough time to let out a breath before my ex-wife's BMW landed on Adams Street with a distant explosion of compressing metal and glass.

"Fuck this!" Lindsey said, pulling the H&K submachine gun from her backpack. She made a quick move above the hood of a Saab and squeezed a burst into the Ford. The shots came so fast they merged into a single, high-pitched thunderclap. Then the Saab's windshield shattered behind a deeper explosion. "They're out of the car," Lindsey said, dropping back under cover. Another deep boom, and the metal door of the car seemed to implode by my shoulder.

"Shit," I said. "They've got some real firepower." I rolled onto the oily floor, searching for their feet. I saw a pair of boots and lined up the sights of the Python, fighting a panic that was about to swallow me up. Hold breath. Exhale. Pull trigger.

The big revolver jumped in my hand, and I heard a high-pitched screeching from the other side of the car. I didn't take the time to check on the guy or his partner. I knew I had bought us only a few seconds. Grabbing Lindsey's wrist, I sprang up and ran hard for the exit stairs. As we ran, she turned and unleashed another round from the submachine gun. The bullets ricocheted against the walls and cars like the devil's calliope, and then my hands hit the blessed metal of the exit door, which opened.

Chapter Twenty-one

We left the scene of a crime. It didn't speak well of the acting sheriff of Maricopa County. But right then I didn't give a damn. Maybe I half-amputated the foot of one of the gorillas who tried to kill us, but I was no closer to understanding who they were, or why they were after us. We went to the hotel because of a call from Captain E.J. Kimbrough, commander of the major crimes unit of the Sheriff's Office. I couldn't believe other cops had set us up for an ambush. But I didn't dare disbelieve it.

We ran, half fell, down the stairs and burst out onto the street like fugitives. We didn't stop running. Survival intuition had kicked in. Lindsey could outrun me any day, she was lighter, more agile, long-legged. But she gripped my hand and we sprinted together. It seemed important to be connected. The dirty concrete of the exit stairs pounded its way into the muscles of my calves. Then we were outside on asphalt and sidewalks. Across Adams, past the sprawled wreck of a BMW 325i, around the back of the old Hanny's building, which had somehow been saved from the demolition crew that made a parking lot of the old central business district. My lungs burned in the cool night air. The streets were empty, but our insides assumed the other goon was right behind us. Sound carries strangely in the Valley, and every distant car engine and closing door echoed with a threatening closeness. Only when we had crossed Jefferson and moved past the halogen glare of the parking garage for Bank

One Ballpark did we feel safe enough to walk. A derelict saw us and went the other way. Our guns were concealed but we must have looked wild. At last, we heard sirens and a chopper going the other direction, to the hotel.

We found sanctuary at Alice Cooperstown, the baseball bar in one of the old produce warehouses on Jackson Street. If the Diamondbacks, Suns, or Coyotes had been playing downtown, the crowd would have been packed out on the sidewalk. Tonight, lucky for us, it was only busy enough for a couple to sit anonymously in the back. He was tall, broad-shouldered, thoughtful-looking. She was dark-haired, fair-skinned, complicated-looking—there was the tiny gold stud in her nostril and the recently fired submachine-gun concealed in her backpack.

"Those guys looked like cops," Lindsey said, finally speaking after the waitress brought us beers, a Negra Modelo for me, a Sol for Lindsey.

I nodded. "You're OK, right?"

"I'm OK," she said. She had a streak of dirt on her fine cheekbone. I reached over and gently rubbed it off. She leaned into my hand, luxuriating in my touch. "Dave, what's going on?" she said. "People are trying to kill us."

"I don't know," I said. "But whoever came after Nixon and Peralta is now after us."

"Dirty cops," she said bitterly.

"Somebody is giving us credit for knowing more than we do," I said. "We know there was some kind of scheme involving Dean Nixon and some deputies, twenty years ago. Presumably it was illegal. We know it was related to the shooting in Guadalupe, and the wild life at Camelback Falls. Somehow that ties into Nixon being murdered and Peralta being shot."

"How?"

"Whoever is trying to kill us thinks we have that figured out, and so we're a threat to them." I sounded like I was giving a lecture on the presidency of Grover Cleveland. I took a deep swig of Negra Modelo.

Lindsey said, "Do you think Kimbrough set us up?"

"No," I said. Then, "I don't think so."

"Think about it, Dave. He was the only person I called Wednesday night when you went to meet O'Keefe. Then somebody tried to take a shot at you. He was the only other person who knew about the logbook, and suddenly Jack Abernathy knew." Concentration bunched up the skin above her brow like pulled linen. "You have to consider it."

I let out a long breath. She was right. But it made no sense. Kimbrough had no connection to the department of twenty years ago.

"That may not mean anything," she said. "He's former DEA, for God's sake. And Bobby Hamid talked about the River Hogs being involved in the drug trade…" She paused, dropped her shoulders. "Am I being nuts, here?"

I took her hand, held it tightly, grateful for skin-on-skin contact with her. "You're not nuts," I said. "What about Abernathy? He worked in the East County. He knew about the River Hogs."

"His badge number isn't in Nixon's book," she said. "No senior officer is there but Peralta."

"I guess. But Abernathy was in Peralta's office the day he was shot. That phone call I got came from an extension in Abernathy's custody bureau. He's been acting strange as hell."

"We can't rule anybody out."

"We've got to find a way to go on the offensive," I said. "I'm tired of being a target. I want to find out what these people are so afraid of."

"We don't even know who to trust."

"Makes me realize why they wanted me as acting sheriff," I said. "I'd be a chump who would be easily thrown off the track, and could be killed if he stumbled onto something."

Lindsey tightened her grip on my hand. "Well, those assholes guessed wrong."

I was finally tasting the beer. It was good to be alive.

"We've got to find the common thread," I said, feeling my linear brain start to kick back in as my survival brain went back into standby. "Peralta and Nixon."

"They can't help us."

I added, "Leo O'Keefe."

"Also out of the picture."

"What about this Jonathan Ledger?" I asked. "We're sure he's dead?"

"If not, he fooled a lot of obituary writers," she said. "He didn't have children. An irony there. We could try to run down ex-wives, that kind of thing."

Lindsey read my expression. She said, "Marybeth."

"Exactly," I said. "She was involved with Leo. She got off and he went to prison. Now we know she was involved with orgies at Camelback Falls, and so was Dean Nixon. She's the key. Can you find her?"

Lindsey smiled, her sensual lips curling. "I can find anybody, Dave. Certainly somebody who's been in the system. Just get me a computer."

I thought about that. It's not like we could go back to the office and act like nothing happened. The jukebox started playing. It was a reggae version of "I Shot the Sheriff." I let out a long sigh.

"We left the scene of a crime," I said.

"Do you want to go back?" she asked.

I shook my head.

Lindsey said, "I never did like that BMW."

When I was eight years old it was important to know all the secret back routes through the neighborhood. We made a map of holes that cut through hedges, trails that ran behind overgrown gardens. The alleys were our Ho Chi Minh Trail on the way to assorted rock fights, trash picking, and other mischief. We guarded our secrets jealously from adults and outside kids.

So it was old memory that led us up the alley between Cypress and Encanto Boulevard. It was pitch dark, and the gravel crunched under our feet. With her black turtleneck, black jeans, and dark hair, Lindsey just disappeared into the night. Only the whiteness of her hands beckoned me. And her breathing—the night was just that still. Mercifully, no dogs barked. Over the back hedge, the house looked just as we left it. A light was on in the kitchen. I had forgotten to start the dishwasher before we left. The ornamental lights in the courtyard were out. The timer shut them off at midnight, and it was closing in on 1 A.M. We crept around the side of the house, between the screened sunporch and the oleanders, where we could peer out onto the street. We had our guns drawn.

It was just early Sunday morning on Cypress Street. Lights were out. Neighbors were asleep, having spent their evenings in activities other than gunfights in downtown parking garages. Lindsey pointed down the street to a darkened van. I hadn't seen it on the street before. The moonless night and the distance made it impossible to see if anyone was inside. We retreated back into the bushes, then went in the courtyard door into the sunporch.

Inside the house, we kept the lights off and didn't speak. We made a quick sweep of the rooms—safe, for now. Lindsey closed herself in Grandfather's office while I sat in a chair and looked out the picture window, the reloaded Python sitting heavily on my lap. A sheen of frost was marching up the windshield of the van. A distant streetlight made it glimmer silver-white. Otherwise, nothing moved.

Around me, the house breathed and creaked in all its familiar old sounds. I could even hear Lindsey's hands doing their warp-speed typing on her laptop. If I thought hard enough, I knew I could have heard Peralta's respirator. The darkness of the living room suddenly reminded me of the night Grandfather died, and how Grandmother and I sat up talking in the dark until the sun finally refilled the room with light. That had been a night in 1976, when I was a rookie deputy and the word of a death in the family had been passed down by the watch commander to my partner. Peralta came back from the phone, gave me the news simply, and drove us back to the station so I could go to the hospital.

I felt a stab of guilt, for leaving the scene of a crime, for endangering Lindsey, for leaving this house, the only material touchstone of my life, so vulnerable. We couldn't stay here long. The BMW's license tag would be run through DMV, and my name and address would scoot across the computer screen that sat on the console of a patrol car. And our only hope seemed to be finding a woman who had watched the carnage at Guadalupe twenty years ago.

The door to the office opened. Lindsey said, "Got her."

Chapter Twenty-two

Kimbrough answered his phone on the third ring. A child was crying in the background, plates were banging, Sunday morning chaos. But after he recognized my voice, I heard a door close and the background noise went away.

"Where the hell are you, Sheriff? Are you OK?"

I just listened for a minute, trying to get a reading on his voice. What did he know? What was he hiding? I was no good at that kind of thing. What I did know was something about Sunday morning chaos. This Sunday morning, I hadn't slept in twenty-seven hours. I knew—I'd counted them. My body ached with cold exhaustion, that peculiar feeling of being disconnected from real life, floating in a sea of disembodied pains and fatigue. I was just tired enough that every fear seemed magnified, and every certainty seemed at risk.

"I'm OK," I said.

"PD found your car downtown," he said. "It looked like it fell out of a parking garage, fifty feet to the street. Tell me you weren't there, and that this was some car theft gone wrong."

"Actually, we were there. I got a call to meet you there."

"What?" His voice jacked up a half octave. "I never…"

"I got a call on my cell phone from the communications center. They said you left a message to meet you on the fourth floor of the Crown Plaza parking garage, at nine P.M. last night. The message said it was urgent that we meet."

"Who told you this?" he demanded. "I never left any message like that."

"Somebody named Deputy Stevens. It sounded authentic. The caller-ID on my cell phone showed a prefix at sheriff's headquarters, just like it was the communications center."

I heard him exhale a long, apprehensive blast of air.

I went on. "When we got there, the garage was deserted. But it was only a minute before two guys drove up in a white Crown Vic. They tried to ram us, and we would have been in the car when it hit the street if we hadn't jumped out and run for our lives."

"Holy shit!" he exclaimed, sounding surprised as hell. "Why would you go up there alone?"

"I had Lindsey."

"Did she kill anybody with that H&K she checked out from the armory?"

"No," I said. "But I got one of the guys in the foot. Check the ERs for reports of 'accidental' gunshots involving white males last night. Anyway, why would I need backup? The message supposedly came from you. I couldn't reach you on your cell phone or home phone to check it out in advance."

"Yeah, well, we had a sick kid last night. I had it turned off," he said. He sounded sheepish. It sounded genuine. "So where are you now? Why didn't you wait around for backup?"

I waited at least a minute, listening to the microwave stations buzz, thinking. Finally, "The two guys in the Crown Vic looked like cops. I guess I don't feel safe in my own department right now."

"I've always believed we had rogue cops involved..." he started.

"Up to two days ago you thought it was Leo O'Keefe," I challenged him.

"OK, OK," he said. "Tell me where you are. I'll send a team of handpicked detectives to guard you."

I ignored him. "How's Peralta?" I asked.

My stomach tightened when he hesitated. He said, "Not good. There's fluid in his right lung. They're worried about pneumonia. He's not responding to antibiotics. I just got back from the hospital."

"There's got to be something that can be done," I said.

"There's something else you should know, Sheriff," he said. "We got back the ballistics report on Nixon. He was murdered with a nine-millimeter pistol."

"So?"

"I asked Mrs. Peralta's permission to test Sheriff Peralta's service weapon."

I almost made an angry bite through my lip. "Did you get a warrant, Captain?"

"I didn't need one," he said simply.

"Even the sheriff is entitled to due process," I snarled. Underneath, I thought about the other pistol in Peralta's desk drawer. Had it been fired? What did I really know? Who did I really trust? Lisa Cardiff was talking in my ear. She wouldn't shut up. Peralta's friend Dean Nixon. What the hell was that? I never knew they were friends.

Kimbrough went on. "We also got the report on the bullets fired at Peralta, and at you the other night at Kenilworth. They are both fifty-caliber rounds, fired by the same weapon. That's heavy-duty sniper stuff. It looks like a hand-load, the shooter going for more power. Lucky for Peralta, the extra powder in the round may have caused the bullet to fragment before it hit him."

"I don't know how lucky he is," I said quietly. My leg muscles burned from exhaustion. But I couldn't sleep.

"Sheriff," Kimbrough said. "Let's talk in person."

"Not now," I said. "I'm going to take a couple of days off, just to have some time to myself."

"This is crazy, Sheriff," he shouted. "What are you doing? Where the hell are you?"

"I'll contact you again," I said. "Find out about the gun-shot reports. And find out if there's a Deputy Stevens in communications."

Kimbrough was talking, but I carefully set the receiver back into the cold metal cradle of the pay phone.

He was a long way off. I was on the other side of the time zone, the other side of the mountains. I stood up from the cramped airport phone corral and looked out the huge plateglass of the airport terminal. The towers of downtown Denver glittered gold and silver in the distance, backed by the Front Range of the Rockies. The mountains were a shock to the plains, a great wall of purple rising up out of the land, filling the horizon. Fingers of winter mist reaching down the dark canyons toward the city. It must be hard to be an atheist here.

I found a seat and tried to distract myself with Niall Ferguson's *The Pity of War*. It's a brilliant thesis of counterfactual history: What if Britain had stayed out of World War I? We would have had a European Union eight decades early, no world wars, and Britain would still be a world power. I was too tired to wrestle down its flaws. So I allowed myself a bit of envy. My ambition had been to write books such as this. Instead, I was the acting sheriff, running out of time. I thought about Lindsey, my constant preoccupation. "I'm not an intellectual, Dave," she had told me. And it was true, in a healthy way. I became close to physically ill over such profanity as post-structuralism and political correctness. Lindsey stayed above those hedgerows, despite her fine mind and incisive ability to detect and cut through bullshit. It was my good fortune that she wanted to spend her life with me.

"History Shamus." Lindsey appeared, carrying bagels and coffee, a mocha for me. "I'd let you give me a backrub but I'd fall asleep right here."

It was Sunday morning, and the airport was subdued. Or maybe it was the sleepless haze I was moving in. I heard flight announcements, but nobody seemed in a hurry. I let the mocha burn my tongue. The coldness evident out the huge windows made me shiver involuntarily.

"You OK?" she said, running her hand up and down my back. I nodded and sipped more scalding liquid.

"Her name is Beth Proudfoot now," Lindsey said.

"Marybeth?"

"She legally changed it in 1989. Unknown if she got Proudfoot from marriage or the phone book." Lindsey lapsed into a cop monotone. "She moved to Denver in 1982. She received a Colorado driver's license in 1983. She applied for a passport in 1989, after her probation lapsed. She visited France and Italy."

"Jeez," I said. "I'm never going to try to hide from you."

She bunched up her mouth in the sexy way that drove me crazy. "You'd better not hide. But when somebody has been through the criminal justice system, it's easier to find them. All I need is that Social Security number, and all databases are mine."

She beamed, unguarded. She looked luminous, in a gray sweater and jeans the color of the cold sky out our airplane window. If she was exhausted it didn't show. I thought about the soft, warm touch of the bottoms of her feet against the small of my back, about that gasp she made when she was close to coming. I wished we were in Denver on vacation, like normal people. I'd love her up in a Jacuzzi overlooking the mountains. But I didn't ski. I had a sheriff's star in my pocket.

"Well," I said, "Let's go get reacquainted with Beth Proudfoot."

Chapter Twenty-three

The airport seemed halfway to Kansas, it was so far from downtown Denver. When I spent a happy summer here years ago teaching twentieth century American history at the University of Denver, the city's airport had been Stapleton International, a five-minute drive from downtown. Now it took five minutes just to get from the car rental garage to Interstate 70.

It was definitely not summer in Denver. Inside our cramped, ugly rental Chevy, the heater struggled against the 10-degree High Plains blast. Lindsey and I both wore sweaters and leather jackets, an unheard-of combination for Phoenix in January, but barely adequate for Denver. As we hit the freeway and sped west, Lindsey asked me if I'd ever been in an orgy. That was easy. I told the truth and said no. Then she asked if I'd ever wanted to be in one. And I could be a guy and still be truthful to the woman I loved. I said, "Not now." Maybe I'm too clever.

"I'm not sharing you," Lindsey said decisively. "Do you think Marybeth—I'd better start calling her Beth—was a willing participant?"

I didn't answer right away, because I was really thinking: *Should I ask Lindsey if she's ever been in an orgy?* I tamped down my primal male insecurities, which could be concealed underneath my urbane academic bullshit exterior. I said, "Why not?"

She was driving, and didn't turn her head as she talked. "I don't know," she said. "Jonathan Ledger looks so creepy in that

photo. So damned self-satisfied." She whipped to the fast lane
to avoid the sudden braking of a minivan. "The girl looks…"

"Coerced?"

"Oh, no," Lindsey said. "She looks more lucid than some of
the others. Nixon looks bombed out of his mind. But she has
this look that's very cold, very nonsensual. And yet very much
aware. Way adult for, what was she, eighteen?"

"I guess the prosecutors thought she looked innocent enough,
if they let her skip out on a cop killing with just probation."

I remembered the terrified young woman with the cheerleader
looks, begging me not to shoot her and Leo as they crawled out
of the backseat that night in Guadalupe.

"That smells like daddy's money," Lindsey said. "But how
does she go from sucking off Jonathan Ledger in a Kodak
moment to being in the middle of a gunfight between two prison
escapees and the Sheriff's Office? I know one of the escapees
was Leo's cousin, but Leo's not in any of those photos. There's
no connection between Leo and Camelback Falls."

Denver suddenly embraced us with warehouse rooftops and a
massive traffic jam. I said, "Hell, how did she get to Camelback
Falls from her safe little upper-class life as a Tulsa teenager?"

The trail to Beth Proudfoot led us into the old neighborhood
north of the Denver Country Club and the booming Cherry
Creek shopping district. Mamie Eisenhower grew up in the
neighborhood, which still boasted neat bungalows built before
the First World War. They had been gentrified into the half-
million-dollar range by Denver's ascent into the New Economy.
Unlike Phoenix, the landscape here was a winter palette of bare,
black tree limbs, livened by the occasional evergreen. No snow
was on the ground, but the gutters were full of brown leaves
and everything had the stiff countenance of winter. Denver and
Phoenix had different histories, too. Denver was a city when
Phoenix was still a dusty farm village. Now Phoenix had long

since outgrown Denver, but Denver still had more of the feel of a city. I liked it.

"There." Lindsey spotted the numbers on the porch of a small but lovingly restored cottage, framed by cedars. She pulled past the house and parked. "That's the most recent address we have. Should we make a courtesy call to the Denver Police?"

"We should," I said. "But I don't particularly want anyone to know we're here."

"Agreed," she said. She reached into the backseat, pulled open her backpack, and retrieved her Glock. She snapped the holster onto the right side of her jeans. Then she slipped an extra magazine into her left pocket. Then she covered it all with her jacket. She said, "Is it better if I check alone while you wait here?"

"You think she remembers me after all these years?" I asked.

"I think you're unforgettable."

"Pardon the unprofessional behavior," I said, leaning over to kiss her. Her lips were warm. "I think I'll go with you." I opened the door to the cold street.

Thirty paces up the sidewalk and five knocks on the door, and there she was. The young blond girl from Guadalupe, right down to her tie-dyed top and tight bell-bottoms. I just looked at her, feeling an odd, out-of-place disorientation.

"We're looking for Beth Proudfoot," Lindsey said.

The girl cocked her head and fixed a look on us with her fine, wholesome features. She said, "And who the fuck are you?"

"Sheriff's deputies," Lindsey said in her hard voice, flashing her badge with a swing that made the girl involuntarily have to follow her hand.

"You got a warrant?"

"Do we need one?" I asked.

The girl gave a heavy sigh and fell into bad posture.

"She's not here," she said. "She's never here."

"She's your mom?" Lindsey asked. She received a semi-affirmative shrug.

"What's your name?" I asked.

She mumbled something that sounded like "Paige." I looked past her into the house. It was fashionably spare, with a few colorful *objets d'art*, large plants, and a Navajo rug. A highly polished string bass sat against one wall, positioned with just the right savoir faire. No books.

"When do you expect your mom to be back?" Lindsey asked.

"How the fuck would I know that?" Paige said, with a heaviness as if we had asked why war is a constant of the human condition.

"You and your mom don't get along?" I asked. She looked at me with a contempt that only beautiful young women can bestow on the mortal world. She didn't have to say anything. I was as vanquished as if I were a pimply seventeen-year-old asking for a date. I tried again, "Where does your mom work?"

Paige looked down at the sidewalk. We were at a standstill and I was freezing. Finally, Lindsey handed her a business card. "Let her know we came by. We'll be back."

We started down the sidewalk when we heard the girl's voice again.

"You're from Phoenix. What's in Phoenix?"

"Your mom used to live there," I said. She just stared at us and shook her head, an older person's shake, sad and knowing, Then she closed the door.

In the car, we ran the heater on high and didn't speak. Lindsey stared back at the house. I ran the zipper of my leather jacket all the way up and still shivered. "What?" I asked finally.

"She reminds me of me at that age," Lindsey said, and she unconsciously gave the same shake of the head.

Chapter Twenty-four

We were just about to pull away from the curb, when the door to the cottage opened and Paige stepped out, now wearing a heavy forest green parka. She waved to us and walked deliberately to the street. She silently held out a card. I rolled down the window, froze anew, and took it. It read: "Beth Proudfoot...Artist" and gave an address I knew was in the Lower Downtown district.

"Thanks," I said.

Her eyes almost seemed to fill with tears. But maybe it was the cold. She said, "If she asks about me, tell her I went to stay with Aunt Amy. But she won't ask about me." Paige spun on the balls of her feet and walked north up the street, then she ran, her hair a bouncing flaxen halo against the fading afternoon light.

I gave Lindsey directions and we drove down Speer Boulevard into downtown. We went almost to Union Station, with its grand beaux arts front and neon roof sign inviting us to "Travel by Train." Then we made a couple of turns and found the address on Beth's business card. When I was teaching in Denver a decade before, these old four- and five-story brick warehouses and offices from the late nineteenth century were close to being torn down. Now LoDo, as it was called, was the hottest neighborhood in the city, a wonderful combination of nostalgia, yuppification, and the desire for dot-com office space. Two blocks away, the façade of Coors Field loomed over the street as if it had always been there. There was nothing like this neighborhood in Phoenix.

We parked and walked across the original cobblestones and remnants of railroad tracks to Beth Proudfoot's gallery. It was nearly four on a Sunday afternoon, but it was open. We stepped into a big, warm-smelling space with hardwood floors, high ceilings, and lots of light. A bell on the door tinkled. I could see a woman in the back—a flash of blond hair—helping a warmly dressed couple. We waited at a distance, grazing from a silver platter with cheeses and fruit, and milling around the sparse displays of what I presumed were artworks by Beth Proudfoot.

My art tastes were eclectic, and if I had money I could really be dangerous. I would add to my tiny collection of Acoma and Santa Clara Indian pottery, start collecting the major impressionists, sprinkle in a few of the postwar moderns, and indulge a taste for Edward Hopper that a recent case had reawakened in me. I didn't know anything. I knew what I liked.

Beth's art wouldn't have worn well with me. A lot of wire, rope, and contractors' flotsam glued to canvases, in crude wooden frames painted in bright primary colors. The frames were the highlight. Inside the frames, it was like high school vo-tech meets *The Twilight Zone*. But I was probably a philistine—cards on the wall announced that ownership of a Beth Proudfoot original began at $20,000. Any hope that her paintings illuminated what happened in Guadalupe twenty years ago, or what happened to Peralta a week ago, were beyond my critical skills.

After a few minutes, the couple left and the woman approached us.

"Welcome," she said, fixing us full-on with one of those you-have-my-full-attention-and-I'm-delighted looks used by salesmen, politicians, and Junior Leaguers. She was tall and very slender, wearing one of those heavy, U-boat commander turtleneck sweaters and a short skirt, both in black. Still, she was shapely, and her movements suggested grace and agility. Her hair was two notches above the color of honey, natural-looking and cut in a rather severe page boy. For all that, the interest was in her face. She had good bones, as Grandmother would say. Atop those bones: no makeup, defiantly aging but still with flawless healthy skin, perfect mouth, and icy blue oval eyes topped by a thatch of vivid gold eyebrows.

"You look like you're from out of town," she said, holding out her arms as if to embrace us. "I can just tell. Now"—she looked me up and down—"you look learned, like you have a tremendous power flowing through you. I would say, you are a writer or an academician, definitely a man of letters." To Lindsey, she said, "And you, with that very dark hair and fair skin and that dangerous intensity in your eyes, you must be an artist-leader of some kind." I felt like we were being conned, but I was sure there were people who got this treatment and were happy to plink down twenty grand for some wire glued to canvas.

"Actually," I said, "We're looking for Beth Proudfoot or Marybeth Watson."

"Maricopa County Sheriff's Office," the artist-leader said, displaying her identification and star.

The high-wattage smile blinked out like a suburban power outage, and something harder and self-aware crept into the woman's face. I would have known that look anywhere. She was Marybeth, twenty years after Camelback Falls.

We didn't waste much more time with pleasantries. "You people never give up, do you?" she said.

I hadn't rehearsed anything. The answers we were after seemed so complicated. The questions we had were inadequate. I just talked. There had been a crime in Phoenix, I said, a shooting of the sheriff and murder of a former deputy. Both men had been on the scene more than two decades before in Guadalupe, when she had a different name and had been arrested after the killing of two cops. Both men had recently come back in contact with that old case.

"What does that mean to me?" she said. "That was a long time ago. The court agreed I was not directly involved. I've had many lives since then. I've tried everything to put distance between that thing that happened and me."

"Is that why you changed your name?" Lindsey said.

Her huge eyes blinked. She walked to the door and turned the lock. She turned the sign to "closed" and faced it to the street. She walked back to us, talking.

"My name is Beth Proudfoot. That is who I am. I am certainly not Marybeth Watson from Tulsa, Oklahoma. I haven't even been to Phoenix for years. It's a depressing place. No soul. The sun shines too much."

"Does the name Peralta mean anything to you?" I asked, fishing. She shook her head, the cool blue eyes expressionless.

"Who is he?"

"He's the sheriff. He was shot almost a week ago. We believe his assailant had something to do with the shooting in Guadalupe years ago."

Lindsey said, "What about the name Dean Nixon?"

"No," she said. Did she say it too fast? On TV the detective always knew those things. In real life, cops were lied to so much it was harder to pick out the really important lies.

I asked, "Tell us about that night in Guadalupe."

Her head went back a bit, but she stayed calm. "I've been through that so many times. Didn't you read my statement, Mr...Detective...whatever..."

"Mapstone," I said. She didn't remember me.

"That's a Welsh name," she said. "David Lloyd George was Welsh."

"He was arguably a failed prime minister," I said, shameless in my worthless book learning.

She stared at me like a fencer who has just removed the mask after a sharp exchange. "Maybe you really should be a man of letters," she said.

"Guadalupe," I prompted.

"We were stupid kids!" she said, her voice carrying back into the spacious room. "We were in the wrong place at the wrong time. It was terrible."

"Why were you there?" Lindsey asked.

Beth sat down on a bench. "Joyride," she said. "Stupid kid joyride. My boyfriend and I hooked up with some bad people.

We didn't know they were escaped from prison. Then those officers stopped us..."

"Why did they stop you?"

"I don't remember," she said. "I was high."

"Are you sure they stopped the car you were riding in?" I went on.

"Yeah," she said. "We were stopped. The guys started shooting. They just shot those officers..."

I went back again. "So you hooked up with these two guys and went riding. What were you doing before you were stopped?"

She didn't answer at first, just stared at the hardwood floors with the closed-in expression of her daughter. All those hidden codes and customs in our genes, whether we wanted them there or not.

"I was high," she repeated. "I don't remember much." Then she stood, reared on me, her face suddenly flushed. "Jesus. It has been twenty-one years! I have tried to forget it! I was a kid!"

"What about Leo?" I asked.

"What about him?"

"When was the last time you had contact with him?"

Her lower lip tightened just a millimeter. "Not for years. He was like a high school boyfriend, for God's sake. Do you stay in touch with your high school girlfriends? He went to prison." She sighed. "My dad made it so I couldn't even talk to him, after we were arrested. Dad never liked Leo. And then life went on..."

"You haven't heard from him lately?" Lindsey asked.

"No." This said with firm shakes of the head. "Of course not"

"Do you know he escaped from prison recently?"

"No," she said, louder. "I didn't know that."

Lindsey said, "Tell us about Camelback Falls?"

"What?" Beth said, a seamless conversationalist.

"Camelback Falls," Lindsey said. "Dr. Jonathan Ledger and his house on the mountain?"

"I don't know what that is," Beth said.

I fished out a card and handed it to her. "You can leave a message on the voice mail if you think of anything," I said. "We're at the Hyatt up the street, and we'll be here a few days. If you remember anything."

"I'm sure I won't," she said. "Would you like to take the cheese and fruit with you?" Sweetness returned. We demurred.

As she let us out into the cold, Lindsey said, "So you've never been on any of the prison pen pal Internet sites, in touch with Leo O'Keefe?"

The winter light cut a harsher profile of Beth. She stared at Lindsey and whispered, "No."

I started down the two steps to the street, but Lindsey held back. She said, "By the way, your daughter said to tell you she misses you, and wishes you'd come home early tonight."

Chapter Twenty-five

Monday morning. It was two hours later in Boston, and my call caught Lorie Pope just as she was going out the door. I asked her if she could talk.

"If you'll give me about thirty minutes to get all these coats off me," she grumped. "Every time I start to miss the East and think I want to live back here, I remember how cold it is in January. What's the temperature in Phoenix now?"

"Probably 75," I said. "But I'm in Denver right now, so I feel your pain. Actually, I kind of like the cold. I just don't have a good coat."

"Well, you're a native Zonie," she said. "You probably thought snow was fallout the first time you saw it."

It was true. I asked her what she was doing on the East Coast. It had only taken several days to find out where she was.

"I'm at Harvard, a Neiman Fellowship." She paused. "It's a journalism thing."

"Sounds like an honor," I said.

"It gets me out of the newsroom for a few months," she said.

"And that keeps me from pissing off the bosses with my daily rebellions."

I told her about my daily rebellions, and she let out a squeal of delight. I could just see her tossing her hair back out of her eyes, smiling that wide white smile and lighting up a Marlboro. "You're the sheriff! I don't believe it! I've been skiing the past week in New Hampshire and I haven't even read the paper online. God, I wish I were there to write that story!" Then she knocked her voice down. "I'm sorry about Peralta. I know he's your friend."

"Thanks," I said. "But as usual, I need your help."

"Anything for my old boyfriend the sheriff."

"Remember that big shootout in Guadalupe in 1979? The two deputies?"

"I covered it, David," she admonished. "Remember, we met when I was covering the police beat?"

"I remember everything," I said "So, what about that case never made the papers?"

"Oh, David, now the bargaining side of my personality is coming out. It's not my best side. Why do you want to know, my love, and what's in it for me?"

"A well-made martini when you get back to Phoenix," I said. "Anyway, you're on a junket."

I knew from the expectant silence that it wouldn't fly. So I told her my story as economically as possible.

"Holy shit," she said. "Are you safe?"

"Yeah," I lied.

"Well, the thing that never got in the paper was the degree of influence exerted by the girl's father, Bill Watson. He was loaded with oil money. And I'm convinced some heavy campaign contributions came to the judge and the county attorney in exchange for the light sentence for Marybeth."

"But she was just a kid, and the record indicates she wasn't directly involved."

"Mmmmm," Lorie said. "So how do you explain the prison sentence for her boyfriend?"

"Daddy's money?"

"Exactly."

"So what do you know about Camelback Falls?" I asked.

She let out a little whistle. "I haven't heard that name in years. It was Jonathan Ledger's house. You know, the sex guy?"

"Did you ever go up there?"

She laughed. "Oh, I had an adventurous youth, but not that adventurous. I did get an invitation to a party there once, but I was busy or had to work or something. It was apparently quite the swinger's place back then."

"I never got those kind of invitations," I said.

"You were too ponderous, my love. All those books and big thoughts."

"So what kind of people went up there?"

"My invitation came from a doctor, a sports medicine guy I was dating. I think I was dating about five men at once then. No, you weren't one of them. Anyway, I got the sense it was a crowd with a lot of money and not much sense. You know, it was the seventies. Anything goes. Ledger kept a salon of beautiful people, and they had legendary parties. That was the rep."

"So no lowlifes, or prison escapees? Or runaways from Tulsa?"

She paused. "David, this is getting way too interesting. Maybe I'd better get on the next plane back."

"What if I told you I'd seen a photo of Marybeth and Jonathan Ledger, and they weren't posing at the South Rim of the Grand Canyon."

"I'd say that's news," she said.

I asked, "What were the River Hogs?"

"This is memory lane. The Hogs were cops, deputies. They were bad news."

"Bad news, how?"

"I'll tell you what I heard, and then I'll tell you what I saw. Remember, I was a twenty-two-year-old kid reporter. If the cops were friendly, they usually just wanted to try to get me into bed. Usually, they were outright hostile. Not only was I the press, but I was a woman."

She went on. "What I heard was that this group of deputies was a kind of force above the law. They looked the other way on things like drugs and prostitution in exchange for protection money. They had the reputation of tough guys, and there was talk they were somehow tied into the Vegas mob. Real muscle.

You didn't want to mess with them. You never knew exactly who they were. That added to the mystique."

"They were the River Hogs?"

"Yes and no. The River Hogs were a joke at first. A bunch of guys would get off duty, buy a few cases of beer and go drink themselves silly down in the riverbed. Big time in the city, huh? When the department brass got wind of it, they tried to shut it down, but the drinking parties always just moved somewhere else. I heard they got really out of hand sometimes, drunken target shooting, bringing along prostitutes and cop groupies, that kind of thing. But there was also this kind of understanding that the way into this shadow group of dirty cops was through these parties. So were they one and the same? I never found out."

"Why didn't I ever know any of this?"

"Oh, David," she said. "You were always in your own world. It was endearing."

"Thanks," I said, feeling not so endearing. "You said you also saw something."

"Yes," she said. "There was this nasty strip of bars down between Tempe and Scottsdale. You remember? Bobby Hamid got his start there. Lots of other sterling citizens. There was one place called Lacey's Lounge. It was totally scummy, but no more so than any other place there. Then one night, just after closing, the deputies raided the place. They shot and killed the owner, a guy named, uh, Jimmy Nance. They said he pulled a gun on them after they identified themselves. And they found a bunch of pot and cocaine."

"So?"

"So, I had done a story on those topless bars a few months before, and I spent some time with this Nance. He was totally neurotic, about guns. Said he'd never own one because he was afraid it would be used on him. David, they planted that gun on him to make the shooting look righteous. He must have backed out on paying his protection money. It's not like the other places got raided. And they got away with it! My editors had zip interest in my pursuing the story."

"So who were the bad cops?" I felt my gut tighten involuntarily.

"I never knew, David."

"Come on, Lorie," I pressed. "There must have been talk. Somebody I know? Somebody I worked with?"

"I swear to God, I don't know."

"What about the two deputies in Guadalupe?"

"Heroes killed in the line of duty," she said. "They were close to retirement. Left behind families. It was the hook for the story for weeks."

"Was it true?"

"David." Her voice tightened with irritation. "I generally try to write the truth."

I said, "Did you know one of them had a failing business on the side? He was really strapped for money when the shooting happened."

She didn't say anything, so I went on. "And did you know those same photos from Camelback Falls show another East County deputy involved in an orgy? That's the same deputy who was murdered last week."

"No, I didn't know any of that," she said. "You're making me feel like an idiot here."

"Welcome to the club," I said.

⟨⟩⟨⟩⟨⟩

I finished up on the phone, then showered and locked up the hotel room. Lindsey had already gone to the public library in search of a T-1 line. We had slept nearly nine hours, snuggled like spoons against the cold world just out the window, interrupted around 3 A.M. for a fierce and satisfying lovemaking. When we woke up, there were six inches of dry powder snow on the ground.

"How did you know Beth had been in touch with Leo via the Internet?" I asked as she dressed and I read the *Rocky Mountain News* in bed.

"I didn't," she said. "It was a bluff. And she fell for it."

Beth had given away something, amid a conversation that seemed to be leavened with lies, shadings. If she wouldn't cooperate, we were stuck. I could go to the Denver cops and begin the process of wrapping her up as a material witness. But there was no time. There was a time deficit. I was a time debtor, and foreclosure was imminent. A week had gone by since Peralta's shooting. It seemed like a year.

I had my own errand. I drove the three miles through plowed streets to Cherry Creek, where the self-help and sexuality section of the Tattered Cover bookstore held several paperback copies of *The Sex Instructions* and *More Sex Instructions*, by Jonathan Ledger. I sat on a bench and leafed through with only mild embarrassment. Hey, I was a kid of the '70s, I had no inhibitions.

Like the other sexuality books of the time, Ledger's books used the trappings of science and liberation to tear down bourgeois hangups and have a grand old time talking about screwing. More than most, however, his books were notable for their frankness and explicit photographs. These were good-looking models in clinical settings, though, not the drugged, flawed, fleshy convivialists at Camelback Falls. Written before the age of AIDS, Ledger's books were evangelical tomes for promiscuity—one chapter was entitled "The Pathology of Faithfulness"—and doing what felt good.

I snapped shut the book as a little girl skipped by. On the back was a photo of Ledger, cropped so you could see only his dramatic black brows and sharply chiseled face rather than the wispy white hair hanging on around his bald pate. "Jonathan Ledger was a researcher, teacher, and lecturer on human sexuality," the type read. "He was born in Utah into a large Mormon family, but broke away from the church as a teenager. Ledger received his Ph.D. in psychology from Princeton, where he conducted pioneering research on female sexuality. As an author, his books spent a total of 87 weeks on the New York Times Best-Seller List. He died in 1984."

I opened the book again and flipped through the photos. Three sets of lovers, attractive sexual artists, demonstrating various positions and flavors. I noticed that the couples didn't stay together. To get Ledger's deeper point of pleasure across, the men and women played musical chairs in different pictures. It would have all been very naughty and forbidden in 1975. Now, it just seemed banal. When I thought of the photos from Camelback Falls—more pioneering research?—it seemed kind of pathetic.

Now I didn't feel deprived. When I was living through those years, I felt like I was missing the greatest party in the history of the world. I could hear my neighbors screwing on the other side of the walls. I could get the sex stories from my friends, male and female. I was so out of it. Now, I didn't miss that past. Now I reveled in the positions and flavors with Lindsey, a woman who loved with enough freshness and sometimes awkwardness that I didn't feel as if she had practiced on dozens of men before me, with the burnout and scars to go along with it. Maybe that was naïve on my part. But whether we made love or just fucked, sex with Lindsey always felt new, and always felt like home.

I looked at the photo of Ledger again. "Tell me something, Jonathan," I said aloud, oblivious to the people around me. Ledger stared at me like a backwoods preacher out to save my soul.

I opened the front pages. A list of his other works. No dedication page. I flipped forward, where it would tell me the copyright dates, the printing history, the ISBN number. The business of publishing. The stuff nobody ever reads.

Then I saw it.

Chapter Twenty-six

It was full dark by 5 p.m. If you looked west, you could see the snowy peaks of the Front Range shimmering in the fading sunlight that had finally broken through the cloudbanks. But in downtown Denver, the snow was churned brown and gray by the traffic, and the streetlights sparkled like dream crystal.

Lindsey was moored to her laptop, so I walked along the 16th Street Mall, all the way down to Larimer Square. The office crowd lingered in warm bars, and snugly dressed young couples shopped and strolled. In a taphouse near Coors Field, I fortified myself with a MacCallen, neat. The jukebox played Sinatra, "One for My Baby." I found myself missing Lindsey, even though she was only half a mile away. And missing Peralta: his capricious temper, his impossible demands, his quirkiness, but all somehow wrapped up in a package that made us feel safe and centered. There was one for Dr. Sharon to expound on.

Safe and centered. In the honest darkness of the bar, I recalled Lindsey's words that morning.

"I thought we were the good guys."

She had said it with a simple sadness as she played with my chest hair, molded against me and warm in the rumpled bedclothes.

"Every cop I ever knew wanted to do good," she had said. "Why else would you put up with the bullshit? The same group of hopeless cases you deal with over and over, when you're on patrol. The harassment from the lawyers and the politicians. I always thought, no matter what, at least we're the good guys."

I had said something forgettable and she had laid her head on my chest, listening to my heart. After a long time, she had said, "I got a call the other day from Yahoo. Can you believe it? They wanted me to talk to them about consulting on security." Then she had gone back to monitoring my heart. Finally: "I would have said no. But this time—Dave, don't hate me—I said I wanted to think about it."

"What do you want to do?"

"I don't know," she had said. Quietly: "We wouldn't have to move. Unless you wanted to live in San Francisco. Maybe go back to teaching and writing. Be safe."

That's where we had left it. When the last precious drops of single malt were gone from the glass, I walked three blocks to the red brick warehouse that held Beth Proudfoot's gallery.

I was mortally afraid of falling on ice. It's not like you got ice balance growing up in Arizona, and I never gained it in the years I lived in cold places. I had already had two near spills, which were almost worse than just going ahead and falling on my ass. So I walked down Blake Street like a little old man, listening like a Minnesota ice fisherman to the ground crunching under my shoes. The giving texture of the snow made a welcome echo. The hard surface of ice was a single note snap that made me wary. My slow pace made it easy for me to gaze into the broad, clean windows of the bright gallery and see the stocky man standing just outside.

He was all arm muscles and thick neck, warmed only by a light black windbreaker. He had a low center of gravity, but stood lightly, bouncing on the balls of his feet, looking at nothing in particular. Beyond him, the gallery was deserted. A purple neon sign glowed in the window in signature script: "Beth Proudfoot." I felt my abdomen tighten.

"It's closed," he said in a slow, heavy voice.

"Why?" I asked.

He stared at me, surprised to be asked a question. His eyes were hazel concrete.

"Closed," he said, more quietly. "Move on." Then he held out a meaty hand toward my chest, almost, but not quite, touching me.

Quicker than he could react, I stepped forward, brought my arms across his forearm and knelt down. It was a neat move I learned years ago in the academy. He grunted and fell to the pavement.

"You can answer my question, or I'll break your arm," I snarled, forcing back all the fears and scruples that civilized living breeds in us. I leaned hard toward the pavement, forcing his arm, and he yelped.

"Who the fuck are you?!" he gasped.

"Wrong answer," I said, and pushed again. I felt his radius start to stretch in a direction it wasn't intended to go.

"Owwwww, shit!" he yelled. "OK, OK, we're here to talk to the bitch. We're on business!" He added, "I'm a cop."

"Bullshit." I reapplied the pressure.

"Ahhh! OK, shit, I'm a bounty hunter. I'm licensed. It's a job, OK? We're after a bail-jumper."

The "we" stuck in my head like a sudden jolt of electricity. I stood quickly and kicked the guy in the stomach, hard. I pulled the Python and jammed it into his nose until blood came out.

"Listen asshole," I said, "You come inside and I'll just kill you. I won't ask a question or give a warning. I'll just blow your ass into eternity. Got it?" He nodded intensely and wheezed, but I knew I had only bought a few seconds.

I jerked open the door; the bell tinkled merrily. I crossed the hardwood floor quickly, heading to the back room. I could hear a woman whimpering, and then the sharp sound of a hand against flesh.

"You'd better give it up, bitch!" a man's voice commanded. Then there was another slap. But that infernal bell had given me away, and before I could reach the archway to the back room, it was filled with bad guy.

"Stop or I'll kill you," I commanded, leveling the Python at his chest. I added the nicety: "Maricopa County Sheriff."

He paused long enough to glower at me with hate. It was the driver from the parking garage. But outside the car, he was huge. Linebacker huge.

"Get on your knees," I said. "Do it!"

He started down slowly. I didn't see a gun on him, but I swear I would have shot him and taken my chances with a review board. He was big enough to kill me with his bare hands. I would have done him. But I caught his eyes sneaking a look over my shoulder, and then I heard the festive tinkle of the bell. I tried to use my peripheral vision and step sideways to counter whatever was coming in the door behind me. That was just the millisecond of distraction he needed to rush me.

In an instant, this human tank was coming for me, yelling like a banshee. It scrambled the circuits in an out-of-shape brain that had spent too many years in comfortable classrooms and bedrooms and drinking establishments, in the luxurious embrace of books and fine dinners and Lindsey Faith Adams. It was not even a second, but it was enough.

A horrific force slammed against my chest—I swear I could hear my ribs crack—and then I was airborne. The tasteful black cylinders of the display lights flew past my eyes, and then I was cruising sideways headed toward a trifold portable wall. Several brightly framed canvases came up to meet my face. I hit hard, pain shooting out of the top of my head. When I hit the floor, it felt like carpenter's nails had been driven into my spine. Then the heavy man-shape in the air above me crashed down.

There was a time fugue where a round black fog started closing down my field of vision and I wasn't there. But one word slammed through my traumatized brain and woke me: gun.

The goon had both his huge hands on the Python, trying to rip it out of my hands. I pulled it toward me, my arms screaming from the strain. The barrel swung toward my nose and I nearly broke my wrist pointing it back out. That fine, ribbed Colt 4½-inch barrel I had paid a premium price for. The steel glinted in the lights. His hands were gigantic and powerful, slowly overwhelming me, but his fingers seemed like delicate little ghouls invading to dislodge my hold on the trigger.

I wiggled like a madman and kneed him in the groin. He didn't even grunt. He just kept up this rhythmic, weightlifter's breathing. His breath smelled like a trash can in July. Suddenly other black arts of the street cop came back to me, and I pulled the gun hard toward me, then quickly pushed it back to him. The force of his grip snapped the heavy revolver back into his face. It crashed across the bridge of his nose, opening a wide, fleshy cut. He let up enough that I could crawl out from under him. He jerked up on his knees, looking like a rattler about to strike. Then I pistol-whipped him again across the jaw. He grunted and fell backwards.

The guy from the doorway sprang at me, but he was slow. I stepped aside and he crashed into a black metal table. The two men crawled around on the floor like large, dangerous roaches. One shook his head violently and tried to stand. I backed away and stepped through into the back room. Beth looked at me with wild eyes.

"Is there a way out the back?" I rasped. She nodded, and led us down a dark passage to the alley. Outside, I grabbed her wrist and we ran like hysterical refugees through the dirty, day-old snow.

Chapter Twenty-seven

Beth didn't want to call the Denver cops. So we ended up back in the hotel room, where Lindsey procured ice. The right side of my face was swollen and felt like an overused pin cushion. My left hand had a nasty cut from some point in the fight. My left shoulder hurt like hell unless I kept it raised as if I were in a perpetual half-shrug. But I felt like I got off easy.

Beth sat in a green upholstered chair, holding an ice pack to her eye. Her shirt had been ripped, and she had a small, deep strawberry-colored cut on one cheek. A crescent bruise was working its way down her perfect jawline. She was wearing black leather pants, and sat with her legs drawn up to her chest. She sobbed quietly.

"We've got to talk, Beth," I coaxed.

"They showed me badges, just like you guys," she whispered. "They said they were going to kill me."

"Did they say why?"

She shook her head and hunkered deeper in the chair. Speaking slowly, she told us how the two men had come in a half hour before I arrived, then waited for her last patrons to leave. When they were alone, the big one shoved her into the back room and started slapping her.

"What did they say they wanted?"

"I don't want to talk now," she said. "I want to go home."

"OK," I said, nursing my own pain. "They may be waiting for you at home."

She looked at me as if I had slapped her. I suggested, "It's time to call the police."

"No," she said, too loud. Lindsey glanced at me. Beth stared at the floor and said, "They wanted Leo. They wanted me to tell them where he was."

"I thought you hadn't talked to Leo," I said.

"You know I did." She smiled unhappily. "We corresponded by e-mail. It was censored by the prison, of course. He was coming up for parole, finally. He was actually hopeful that this time he might make it."

"When did you last hear from him?" I asked.

There was a commotion in the hall and my stomach knotted up, sending a sharp pain into my ribs. Lindsey sprang up, drew her Glock, and moved lightly to the door, which was already bolted. She just shook her head. The noise died down. I asked Beth the question again.

"I got the last message from him just before Christmas."

"Did you have any sense he was planning an escape?"

"No." She shook her head vehemently, tossing her fair hair, pushing it back with an agitated hand.

"Why would he escape if he thought he might get parole?" Lindsey asked, returning to sit on the bed.

"I don't know," Beth said.

"Really?" Lindsey asked.

"Yes, really." Beth stared daggers at Lindsey.

"So what did you tell these tough guys when they wanted to know where Leo was?" I asked.

"I told them I didn't know," she said, lightly touching a finger to the cut on her cheek. The motion made my face throb.

"So Leo hasn't contacted you since he escaped?"

"No, damn it. He hasn't. Why would he come to Denver if he was in Phoenix last week?"

Lindsey and I kept poker faces. But Beth was quick, if dulled a bit by being beaten up. She realized instantly we hadn't told her that Leo was seen in Phoenix. She muttered an obscenity and stared into her lap.

"What do you want from me?" she demanded in a raw voice.

"The truth would be a good starting point," I said.

She stared out into the room for a long time. Then, quietly, she said, "Tell me about you guys. I'm usually very intuitive about people, and you two definitely don't look like cops."

I'd seen Peralta break down hard guys in the interrogation room. He could browbeat, threaten, manipulate, and sometimes be the most compassionate man in the city. But his interview skills always had a beginning, a middle, and an end designed to wear down the suspect. He never let the suspect take control, as Beth had just done. But I went along with it.

"Lindsey works with computers." I said. "I'm the acting sheriff."

"You're the sheriff?" she asked, with enough incredulity to sting my ego. "How did that happen?"

"I've been asking myself the same question," I said quietly. "The real sheriff is badly wounded. I told you that yesterday. I guess the county brass figured I'd be the safest choice to fill in for a few days."

"You're a cop?" she demanded.

"Not really. I work on old cases. I'm a historian by training, and I used to teach. I kind of landed in this job three years ago."

"Unbelievable," she said, but seemed pleased with this information.

"So tell us what really happened," I prodded.

"They told me they'd kill me if I said a word!" She looked at me straight on, fear in her eyes.

"Tonight?"

"No." She shook her head vehemently. "No, damn it. Twenty years ago…" She tried to slow her breathing. "You don't know anything, do you?"

We just sat and watched her. The room smelled of winter heat. Beth wrapped her arms around her legs and talked in a slow voice. "That night in 1979, when the shooting happened. It wasn't what you think. Billy and Troyce had a deal with those old cops. They stole twenty pounds of cocaine from the evidence room, and Billy and Troyce were going to break it down and sell it. They were going to split the profits."

My head felt heavy from the swelling around my eye, and from Beth's words. I said, "Beth, these were decorated deputies, killed in the line of duty on a traffic stop."

"Yeah, right." She laughed. "I was there, OK? I saw what happened."

Lindsey asked, "How did all this come about? How did Billy and Troyce know the deputies?"

"I don't know," she said, too quickly. "They knew a lot of bad people."

"How did you get there?" Lindsey wanted to know.

"They picked up Leo and me, to go riding," she said. "We didn't know what the hell was going on. And once we realized, it was too late to bail out. So we were just supposed to meet these cops in Guadalupe, take the stuff and go. That was it."

I said into the pause, "What went wrong?"

She shook her head. "I don't know for certain. We stayed in the car. But I could see Billy and Troyce start shouting. It got really heavy. Then Billy ran back and got this rifle, and started shooting. We ducked down in the back seat. I just knew we were dead."

She readjusted the ice on her jaw and went on. "Don't you get it? The cops were dealing drugs. There was twenty pounds of cocaine in that cop's car that night."

"But you said you were threatened about talking," I said. "Who threatened you?"

"After we were put in jail, this detective talked to me. He said if I ever talked about what I'd seen that night, they'd find me and kill me. He told me what I was supposed to say, and gave me a statement to sign. The statement said we'd been stopped for speeding, and Billy and Troyce opened fire on the cops for no reason. That's not at all what happened."

"Did you tell your lawyers any of this?" Lindsey asked.

"Are you nuts?" Beth said. "This guy said they'd kill me, and I believed him. I always hated having a rich father, but that time I let him rescue me, and I never talked about what happened."

I asked, "What did this detective look like?"

"I don't know," she said, flustered. "A white guy. Average. Dark hair."

"What happened to the cocaine that night?"

She sighed and stretched out her legs. "You got anything to drink?"

There was a bottle of Glenlivet on the dresser. I rounded up three glasses and poured everybody two fingers. Beth bolted down the scotch in one slug. Then we sat in silence, listening for God knows what coming down the hallway. A soft murmur of downtown traffic penetrated the window.

Finally, Beth said, "Another cop took the coke."

We didn't say a word, so she went on. "He was big. Hispanic."

Every one of my aches throbbed deeper, but I just sat there and nursed the Glenlivet. I wished for the more expensive scotch I had enjoyed earlier in the evening, when my overly complicated life was a little less complicated than it had since become.

"Why don't you walk us through what you remember," Lindsey suggested.

"I was in the back of a squad car, handcuffed," Beth said. "But I had a good view. This Hispanic cop walked to the trunk of the first cop car. The trunk was already open. And he took out the coke, and put it in his car."

"How do you know it was the cocaine?" Lindsey asked.

"I saw it," Beth said. "The old cops had pulled it out and showed it to Billy and Troyce before things turned bad. It was in this grocery bag. And after...well, this big Hispanic cop took it."

"Beth," I said. "You'd just been through a shootout. You were afraid for your life. Are you sure you remember that correctly?"

"That's when your senses are at their peak," she said. "Look"—she sighed—"the big cop took it, he and his partner, a tall Anglo. A younger guy. He was the son-of-a-bitch who threw me down in the dirt and handcuffed me."

I just stared into the golden liquid, wondering what her game was. She said, "Don't you see why this could get me killed? And

Leo? That deputy was named Peralta. I saw his photo in the newspaper after I was arrested, and I never forgot that name. And I know he's your sheriff now. So how the hell are you going to protect me, professor?"

Lindsey glanced at me, but I had no grand plan to telegraph back. I said, "Will you testify about this?"

"Are you nuts?" She laughed. "When those two gorillas showed up tonight, it was just like that detective had told me twenty years ago. If I talked, they'd find me and kill me."

"What about the FBI, the U.S. Attorney?" I said. "Nobody can touch you there."

"I'll think about it," she said.

The phone rang. I reached over and picked it up, but it was just empty air. I set it back into the cradle. A flash of alarm registered in Lindsey's dark blue eyes. I tried not to feel paranoid.

The phone rang again, an efficient electronic trill. I watched it for a moment, let it ring three times and picked up.

"Mapstone," an unfamiliar voice said. A male voice. Wait, had I heard that voice last week on the phone in Peralta's office? The voice said, "You're all dead."

"We've got to go," I said, dropping the receiver, tossing aside the ice pack and standing. Lindsey had read the situation and was already moving.

"What?" Beth shouted. "What?"

"There's no time," I said. "We're in danger. We're going to the Denver police."

"No!" she shouted, her voice jagged. "I have a business here. I can't have this. Jesus, I have tried to get away from all this for twenty years!"

Her face worked in agony. Her jaw tensed and eased, tensed and eased. She jumped up. "OK, I'll go back to Phoenix. I'll talk to your U.S. Attorney. Just talk."

There was no time. The phone's insistent trill still seemed embedded in the walls. We grabbed coats, guns, and bags, checked the hallway, then carefully went down the fire stairs and out into the cold.

Chapter Twenty-eight

We held a quick strategy session out in the car, as I drove around the snow-shiny streets south of downtown to ensure we were not being followed. Lindsey was sure the bad guys had tracked us down through our county credit card transaction. "It's easy to hack into. Anybody can do it," she said to a man who gets tangled up in a web browser. If they were that savvy, they'd know our return flight and be waiting. Even if we changed the flight, all they had to do was stake out Denver flights arriving at Sky Harbor. I didn't want a dead witness, even if I didn't like what she was saying.

So we decided to drive back. It wasn't that simple. I didn't trust our mid-sized Chevy over the mountains, so we went back to the airport to rent a four-wheel-drive. I used my American Express, which Lindsey predicted might slow the bad guys down for a few hours. I had a hard time believing the same gang that had sent the pro-wrestling dropouts to Beth's gallery was capable of hacking the financial services network, but I also didn't have a good explanation for how they found our hotel room.

By 8 P.M., we were aboard one of those huge Chevy Suburbans I had vowed never to drive. But its size and above-the-traffic view were reassuring. If we had to do battle, we were now in a battleship. We came back through Denver and stopped at a mall to buy Beth a coat and some essentials. I vetoed going back to her house, for safety's sake. Her daughter, Paige, had gone off Sunday to stay at Beth's sister's house in Estes Park, so there was nobody else to rescue.

While Lindsey and Beth shopped, I stood at a pay phone by the mall entrance and called Kimbrough. It was a short conversation: I told him I was coming back to the Valley with a material witness, who would only agree to talk under the protection of the feds, and I told him about the encounter at the gallery where the tough guy had identified himself as a bounty hunter.

"That makes sense," Kimbrough said. "We found a report of a guy who came into St. Joseph's ER on Saturday night with a gunshot. He said it was self-inflicted. But they called Phoenix PD, and they arrested the guy. Name of Jim Caldwell, and he's a licensed bounty hunter. Get this, he worked with Dean Nixon, running down bail jumpers. They had a long record of violent situations."

"So where is he?"

"The lockup at County Hospital," Kimbrough said proudly. "He's not talking, but he will. His left ankle was shattered by a .357 round, and his foot was nearly blown off."

"That's nothing compared to what he would have done to us," I said. "So tell me this guy was never a deputy sheriff."

"I can do that," Kimbrough said. "This guy's just some loser. But you need to know, I talked to Internal Affairs today."

"OK." A laughing flock of teenage girls flew by, giggling and talking. I switched the receiver to the other ear, sending my left shoulder into a spasm of agony.

Kimbrough said, "They interviewed a retired deputy named Collins, lives out in Sun City. He's scared he's going to lose his pension if he doesn't cooperate. So he starts telling this story of how twenty pounds of cocaine disappeared from the evidence room the week before the shootout in Guadalupe. He says it was checked out for a court appearance by Deputy Virgil Bullock, and never returned."

"We need to revisit the records of Bullock and Matson," I said. "Maybe they weren't the heroes everybody thought."

"You'll have their families go crazy," he said, "but we've already started. Their badge numbers are in Nixon's little book.

Petty amounts of money. But this cocaine theft is very troubling I'm going back to look through the evidence logs from that time period."

I just listened. So at least part of what Beth had been saying might be true. I thought about Bobby Hamid's question: What happened after the shooting?

"Sheriff," Kimbrough said, "You need to know people are asking about you. The brass. Davidson and Abernathy, IA. The feds. And Sharon…."

"How…?"

"It's not good," he said. "He's still got brain activity, but he's in a deep coma. He might wake up tomorrow, and he might never…"

"I'll be back in Phoenix tomorrow," I said.

"What's this witness all about?"

"It's about Guadalupe," I said. I didn't tell him she was a lethal witness, lethal to Peralta, maybe even to me—the "tall Anglo partner" who was there when the big Hispanic deputy took the cocaine. There would be time enough for that.

"You could try trusting me," he said quickly.

"I do," I said. "That's why I risked making this call."

We drove west, scaling the Front Range on US 285. It seemed safer to take secondary roads, and a few inches of snow were nothing for Colorado snowplow crews. The highway was clear. It was also nearly deserted. When I lived in Denver, I had seen summer weekend traffic stacked up for miles heading back into the city from the Rockies. But on this weeknight, we had the two wide lanes nearly to ourselves as the elevation rose and my ears popped, and popped again.

Beth was a talker, especially once she was warm in a coat again. She sat in the front seat beside me, but turned to face Lindsey.

"Why do you have that?" she touched her nostril, to indicate Lindsey's nose stud.

"Because I want it," Lindsey said.

"I'm an artist," Beth said. "I like the idea of art on the human body. It just doesn't seem like a cop thing to do. I guess you do it so you can work undercover."

"No," Lindsey said simply, and looked back out at the black mountainsides and forest flying by. I remembered the first time I saw Lindsey, brainy and leggy and quietly intense, with that tiny gold stud in her nostril. She asked why I didn't smile. "I'm smiling inside," I said. She smiled at me and said, "There are no ironic deputies." It was the start of a fine romance. I could have told the story of the nose stud, how Lindsey had gone out and done it as a teenager the weekend after her father died, how she told me she needed to feel something amid the crushing numbness. But Beth didn't need to know any of that.

"You two are together," Beth said.

"Why do you say that?" I asked.

"It's the way she looks at you, and the way you look at her. It's not hard to see."

I said, "You never told us why you knew Leo was in Phoenix last week. We didn't tell you that."

That shut her up, and the miles clicked by. The sky glowed a dull white against the tent poles of pine trees. The speedometer needle stayed steady on 60. No need to take a chance with black ice. I was taking enough chances. On the lam from my own department. Transporting a witness across state lines under a shaky justification. Unable even to arrest the person who shot Peralta. Unwilling to go back to Beth's recollection of the cocaine and the Hispanic deputy. Who the hell was I? Just the idiot they got to be acting sheriff.

We'd just passed the sign for Como when Beth spoke again.

"I knew Leo was going to Phoenix because he told me he was going to," she said, "When I told you I hadn't communicated with him since December, that was a lie. He called me. It was a Sunday night, a week ago."

Before Peralta was shot, but maybe not before Nixon's murder.

"He said he was out of prison. He didn't say he had escaped, and I didn't want to know, OK? But he said he was going to the Valley."

"Did he say why?" Lindsey said.

"He said he needed to talk to someone who could help him clear his name. That's all he said."

"And the next thing, we show up at your door yesterday asking about him?"

"No." She shook her head. "I got a call last week. It was Wednesday. From your office. Somebody from the Maricopa County Sheriff's Office, asking if I knew where Leo was. That's all he asked. That's why I said 'You guys never give up' when you two showed up. And because I knew who your sheriff was, it scared me."

I watched the road ahead. I knew it was too much to ask if she had gotten a name from this MCSO voice who called. And she hadn't.

Beth was slowly getting her story straight. Or some kind of story straight. So I decided to push my luck.

"Beth, remember when you told us you didn't know what Camelback Falls is?"

"Yeah," she said, guilelessly. "What is it?"

"It's a house, on Camelback Mountain," I said. "And you would have to know that, considering we have some photos of you in the house, in some interesting circumstances."

Out of my peripheral vision I watched for a reaction. She just stared into the windshield, her face sheltered by the darkness of the road.

I went on. "I also assume you would know the name Camelback Falls because I was reading one of Jonathan Ledger's books today, and the book lists Beth Proudfoot as the copyright holder."

She said, very quietly in a glassy, precise voice, "You fucker."

Chapter Twenty-nine

She was Marybeth when they met. Just a kid, saying she was eighteen. Men looked at her, they had since she was eleven. She knew she had that power; sometimes it bored her and sometimes it repulsed her. Most of the time she liked it, when it didn't scare her, what she could do to men, what they were willing to do for her. Still, her only boyfriend had been Leo, awkward, skinny Leo, who rescued her from Tulsa and her father. But that was all prologue to Phoenix and Jonathan and Camelback Falls.

She was Marybeth, and she had an accent. It didn't stand out in Tulsa, but she felt like a hick every time she opened her mouth in Phoenix. There are lovely Southern accents, especially attached to pretty girls, but the Oklahoma twang is not one of them. Jonathan picked it out that day, when he walked into the toy store at Scottsdale Fashion Square, a job she had taken to help pay the rent. He said he liked her voice.

He had a voice as rich as his brown, ruddy skin. Man's skin, used to the sun. As rich as the onyx brown eyes that looked at her so intensely. He wanted a teddy bear. He bought a big one with a red vest and the softest fur in the store. His hands were very large. Then he asked her to go for a drink when she got off work, and she said yes. She was living with Leo. "But I just felt like this whole world was about to open up to me," she recalled. "So I rolled the dice."

She slept with Ledger that night. They went up to his big house overlooking the city. She had never seen such a sight before. She didn't know he was a best-selling author, or a controversial researcher of human sexuality. She didn't know he was nearly forty years older than her, and she certainly didn't know about the parties. All she knew was that a world had been opened to her, adult, free, intoxicating.

"I woke up a little before dawn," she said, "and I walked to this window overlooking the city. It was a whole wall of glass. I could see the city lights, all the way to the far mountains. It was like this enormous jewel. It just shimmered with possibilities. I realized I was totally naked, just standing there in that window, and it was the best goddamned feeling in my life."

I couldn't resist. "I thought you said Phoenix has no soul."

"I was a kid," she said. "I was beguiled by the city lights."

That was in January 1979, five months before the shootout in Guadalupe. She stayed another day and night, and then Jonathan sent her home to Leo.

"He said he didn't want to be tied down with one lover," she said.

"Sounds so seventies," Lindsey said from the back seat.

"I didn't feel used," Beth said, almost dreamily. "Jonathan invited me back. So I figured I passed the test. I was so inexperienced then, I wasn't sure if I knew what do. So in a week, Jonathan called me at the toy store and we went on another date."

That date was to San Francisco, to a book signing. Marybeth was the daughter of a millionaire, but her life had been sheltered and very middle class. Piano lessons, church, and two trips to Europe to see museums. San Francisco with Jonathan was a different level of existence. He took her to expensive restaurants, made her feel like a wined-and-dined lady. He let her stand off to the side as he gave interviews and signed books. He met with the editors of *Rolling Stone* and went drinking with a crowd that included San Francisco Giant players, *Sports Illustrated* writers, a TV anchorman, and a jazz musician whose name she couldn't remember. Jonathan Ledger was famous. Before that, the only famous man Marybeth had met had been the governor of

Oklahoma. Indeed, Jonathan was at the zenith of his fame—he embodied the age and the age rewarded him.

That was when the drugs started. At the parties, pot and cocaine were as natural as taking a drink of water. It was impolite to say no, and there was still something of the Tulsa debutante in Marybeth. But the first time she ever sniffed coke and then sneezed the line off into oblivion, she knew she had touched something she was hardwired to love.

"So Jonathan turned you on to coke?" I asked.

"Oh, no, I found that on my own. He was actually protective. He didn't want me to rush in."

"What a responsible adult," Lindsey said. "He'll sleep with a seventeen-year-old girl on the first date, but he won't force her to snort cocaine."

At that point, Marybeth became a regular at Camelback Falls. The parties just naturally morphed into sex parties after a few hours. It didn't shock her. It felt good. She felt in control. Maybe too much. She took up with one of Jonathan's rich friends, a former basketball star named Sam. Jonathan had introduced her, slowly, to sex with other men. But she started seeing Sam outside the jurisdiction of Camelback Falls. It made Jonathan jealous. "It was the first time I realized the way power shifts back and forth in a relationship. I finally had the power."

What she meant, I realized, was the power over Jonathan. "He was very brilliant," she said, "and very gullible and lazy. He did his best work with me."

So she kept Jonathan on a string, and played with Sam, and was the center of the parties at Camelback Falls. "It was a beautiful time, whether you believe it or not," she said. "The people were beautiful. It was very free. Very...noble. I guess it couldn't last."

"Where was Leo at this point?" I asked.

"He was still living in our shithole apartment on Roosevelt Street. Driving a cab all night long, nearly getting killed half the time."

"Did he ever go to Camelback Falls?"

"No." She half-smiled. "This was the elite. Not in his class."

"So he went away."

"I saw him sometimes. Stayed with him sometimes. I felt sorry for poor Leo."

"Sorry enough to go riding that day in Guadalupe?"

There was a long silence, and then she said, "It didn't happen that way. You see, Jonathan was always attracted to the dark side. He was a very spiritual man, but the itch he couldn't scratch was very dark. There's a connection between violence and sex, but thousands of years of civilization tries to tamp that down, keep it locked in its dungeon. It's the opposite of romantic love, but it's just as real. Maybe more so. Jonathan was very attracted to that, so some of the people at Camelback Falls were rough, dangerous types."

"Like Billy McGovern and Troyce Meadows?"

"Yeah. They were the dangerous, sunburned cowboys, really gorgeous men. But you also had the sense they would kill, take what they want. Not some movie but the real deal. You could almost smell it. That was very attractive to Jonathan."

"So how did these guys get there?" I asked. "I read somewhere that one of them was Leo's cousin."

She laughed. "The media. God, what morons. And you call yourself a historian? That was the story Daddy's lawyers gave to the publishers and TV station owners. See, Billy was my cousin, not Leo's. The black sheep of the family, you might say. Jonathan was fascinated by those two, real prison escapees. It was all very arousing, especially for the female guests. The allure of the outlaw, don't you know."

I let that all sink in before asking her the next question.

"Dean Nixon?" she said. "Oh, he was there. He was another one of the people Jonathan collected. He had certain attributes… well, you've seen photos, so you know. And then he turned out to be pretty good at supplying drugs for Jonathan's parties out of the cops' evidence. Jonathan could have paid for all the coke in Bolivia. But getting it that way was more fun to him."

"So in Guadalupe," I said, "that twenty pounds of cocaine was destined for parties at Camelback Falls."

"I don't think so," Beth said. "I think Dean and Billy and Troyce had reached some understanding, and they were working together. They were going to sell the drugs on the street."

"Until that big Hispanic deputy took them," I said. "Did he ever show up at Camelback Falls?"

"No, never saw him before," she said. "But most cops are dirty." She added, "No offense."

"What about the detective who threatened you? Did he come there?"

"No, Mapstone. You've got to understand the makeup of Jonathan's circle. Dean was there only because Jonathan collected him."

"Do you know Dean has been murdered?"

Beth was silent.

"And so all this went away after the shooting? Daddy rescued you and you went back to Tulsa?"

"I did for awhile," she said. "I went to college at Vassar, like Mother wanted. The parole was very generous. So it was easy to drop out and come back to Phoenix."

"Why?" Lindsey asked.

"Jonathan," she said. "Don't you see, Jonathan loved me. I was with him to the end. The parties trailed off after 1980, and I never saw Dean Nixon after I came back to Phoenix. Jonathan left his estate to me, including the books. Really pissed off his ex-wives. But they didn't sit with him as his life ended, either, did they?"

She stared out at the darkness. "He had beautiful eyes," she said. "Paige got his eyes."

Chapter Thirty

Lindsey took over the driving, and we crossed the Continental Divide in silence. There seemed to be nothing left to ask or say. Beth fell into an exhausted sleep. She dream-drummed her long fingers on the thigh of her leather pants. I stretched out in the back seat and tried to rest. Every position was painful, and every notch my body relaxed caused a new ache to emerge. The Suburban was dark and warm, filled with memories.

My old job is nearly obsolete. The idea that historical facts can be found and historical truths can be taught is hopelessly out of style in universities. Now they talk of poststructuralism, many voices, many truths. All that old stuff is part of the oppression of the white male patriarchy. Even the name of my great academic love is disgraced: history, as in the sexist term "his-story."

As I pondered my story, I realized again why it's nearly impossible to write a credible history of events you have lived. Unless you're Churchill, and I am definitely not. Assessing and interpreting the past is not like a martini, best drunk just after it's made, with the little ice crystals still floating amid the gin, just like they make them at Durant's. No, real history needs time and distance. And I had neither.

Beth said she sat in a patrol car and watched Peralta remove a sack of cocaine from Matson and Bullock's trunk. I had been there, too, and I saw no such thing. But, as any street cop can tell you, a dozen people can witness the same event and come away with a dozen different recollections. Bobby had asked what happened after the shooting as if the answer held important keys to everything that had happened over the past week.

As the black mountain road unfolded, I pushed into my memories. The dust in my mouth that night. Dust mingled with gunsmoke. It was a strange taste. I had barely avoided death, but that was a thought for later. We were cops. There was the job to do. Four dead men on the ground. Peralta took the weapons from the suspects and handcuffed them, even though they were a long way from life. They lay bleeding into the desert soil. I checked for pulses on Matson and Bullock. They were cool to the touch. It was the first time I had seen dead cops. Their uniforms were the same as mine, only theirs were covered in blood and shredded by bullets. I closed Matson's eyes, and spread plastic disposable blankets over each body. The plastic blankets were yellow and clung together like Glad wrap.

We found Beth and Leo. I did throw them into the dirt and handcuff them, that was true. They were lucky to be alive. Cops are jumpy when people have been shooting at them, and I wanted these suspects down and quiet for their own safety. Then Nixon got there. As always, a pack of cigarettes formed a distinctive lump in the pocket of his uniform shirt. He wore racy sunglasses, and carried a long-barreled .38 revolver. We stuck Beth and Leo in the back of his cruiser and read them their rights.

Where was Peralta? I couldn't remember. I stared out the window of the Suburban. Old logging roads came out to meet the asphalt of the highway, then disappeared back in the primeval forest. The yellow line of the road was bright and unbroken, striped on the slick blackness of the asphalt. The road behind us was empty. A brief flurry shot big, phosphorescent flakes against the windshield. I reached out and stroked Lindsey's hair as she drove. Her hair was glossy and soft, and it brushed luxuriously against her collar.

She said, "It's going to be OK, History Shamus," and reached back to hold my hand.

Counterfactual history. What if I hadn't let Peralta keep talking to me that afternoon at Immaculate Heart Gym—what if he had moved out of the range of the sniper? What if Sharon hadn't sent me to his office for the insulin—"Mapstone—Camelback Falls"? What if twenty years before, Peralta had not been there with his shotgun when I came face-to-face with Billy McGovern?

The enormous Chevy Suburban hurtled us forward to an unknown historical destiny. But what about May 1979? Where was Peralta while Nixon and I were arresting those kids? I couldn't remember. I made myself run through the events again. I had all night.

⟨⟩⟨⟩⟨⟩

By the time I woke up, the sun was grudgingly coming up on our backs. The San Juans vaulted up like ice-cream-topped fantasy mountains out the lefthand side of the truck. The landscape looked eternally cold.

We pulled into Durango, ordered breakfast at a greasy spoon on the main drag, and Beth announced that she wanted to go back to Denver.

"Why didn't you say that last night?" Lindsey said crossly. "I guess we can put you on a Greyhound."

"I changed my mind, OK?" She leaned forward on the table, glaring at Lindsey. "I'm not under arrest, am I?"

"No, you're not," I said, downing three aspirin to try to stop all the aches and pains from last night's fight. "You just had a couple of guys trying to kill you. I expect they won't stop trying."

She swirled her scrambled eggs and said nothing. I winked at Lindsey, and we all ate in silence. In thirty minutes we were on the highway again, heading southwest. Beth didn't ask to be dropped at the bus depot.

The highway shimmied past Four Corners and we were back in Arizona. My jurisdiction was a little more solid, even if my sense of how all this would turn out was getting shakier every mile we got closer to Phoenix. I drove while Beth, in the passenger seat, stared out at the vast red landscape. In the far distance, the mesas of Monument Valley sat like gameboard pieces. I thought about Peralta and my stomach ached.

When Beth finally spoke, I couldn't make out the words.

"I said," she repeated, "do you have panic attacks?"

I glanced over at her. She didn't look hostile, just wondering. I said, "No. Why do you ask?"

"The way you were breathing," she said. "The expression on your face. I used to have them."

I felt scrutinized, invaded. I said nothing but was acutely aware of all my bodily imperfections ticking toward the last tick. Shit.

Beth went on. "I'm going back to Phoenix because of you, Mapstone. You're human. You're not a real cop, and I mean it as a compliment. You probably even read books. So I'll make a leap of faith on you."

I felt like I should say something, so I asked her how she got into art.

"I've always been creative. My parents didn't see it. Leo did."

"How did you meet Leo?"

"We met at band camp. We were both sixteen. Can you believe that?" She kicked off her shoes and put her stockinged feet on the dashboard, stretching into the seat. Her legs seemed very long and slender in the black leather pants. "I played clarinet and he played trumpet. He came from this little crossroads in southeast Oklahoma called Calera. Dirt poor. His dad ran off after he was born, and his mom died young. He was brought up by his older brother, and then he died, too. Leo had that kind of luck. The weirdest thing, he loved jazz: Coltrane, Herbie Hancock, Mingus. A funny-looking little guy. I was taller than he was."

"Doesn't sound like a good catch for a Tulsa deb," I said.

"That's why I had to seduce him," she said, running an agitated hand through her wheat-colored hair. "I hated my life. I hated the preppy assholes my age with all their money. All my dad's friends who were secretly trying to get me into bed. Leo was just this sweet, gentle, goofy… poet. He wanted to save a damsel in distress, so I let him save me."

"How did you get to Phoenix?"

"We drove," she said. "We drove in this piece of shit orange Opel he bought down on Red River. We escaped from Tulsa and my family. It was very romantic and dramatic. We were going to L.A. But the alternator went out between Tucson and Phoenix, and there we were."

"No money?"

"I took some savings, but I didn't want Daddy's money. Not then, anyway."

"So you were just going to get married, have babies, live a conventional life?" I asked.

"You don't think when you're seventeen," she said. "Hell, sometimes you don't think when you're thirty-nine. I knew I was using Leo to get the hell out of Tulsa, and having this kind of gritty, working-class adventure. Sometimes I was very romantic and dreamy. I took a job at a mall. He had this dream of opening a coffeehouse where he could play jazz. Can you believe that, in 1978?" She gave an unhappy laugh. "He was ahead of his time."

"You make him sound pretty nice," I said. "Yet he's been in prison for almost twenty years. We have child murderers who get out sooner than that."

"That's your so-called system of justice, Mapstone. Don't ask me. The families of the dead deputies opposed his parole every year. I'm sure the corrupt cops didn't want to take a chance of him getting out and talking to the media."

"But Leo killed a man in prison," I said. "He couldn't have been that gentle."

She was silent for a long time, and when I looked over, her face was red and turbulent.

"Beth, you're going to have to talk about these things. That's the only way to help me stop these people who are trying to kill you." Yes, me the grandiose hero with panic attacks. I added, "It's the only way to help Leo."

"This is hard, OK?" she said. "I have a lot of guilt, OK? I guess Leo killed a man. I tried not to think about it. We tried to correspond for a couple of years, but it just got too hard." She stared over at me. "Do you understand, he was small and young, and they just threw him in with the worst criminals?"

I asked quietly, "He was attacked?"

She nodded. "I'm sure things were even worse than he told me in his letters."

‹›‹›‹›

The Navajo Reservation enfolded us. We skimmed noiselessly through Monument Valley, the mesas and buttes seen in a hundred movies and TV commercials so much more stunning in reality. Patches of snow congregated on the ledges of the big rocks. The sky was a heavy, endless blue. The miles passed quickly at 85.

Beth said, "So you saw pictures of me at Camelback Falls?"

I nodded.

"I was a cute kid, huh?"

"Yeah, Beth. No question."

"Did the pictures make you hot, Mapstone?"

I didn't respond or look at her. The road vibrated up through the Chevy's suspension.

Beth said, "Do you want me to suck your cock?"

The words hung in the air between us. I unconsciously glanced in the rearview mirror. Lindsey was asleep, zipped up in her jacket, sprawled out in the backseat.

Beth said, "Your little friend back there doesn't have to know. It would be hotter to do it with her asleep just a few inches away"

"No," I said.

"Oh, come on Mapstone," her voice trilled. "What were you doing in the seventies when I was partying at Camelback Falls? I bet you wish you were there." She reached her hand across the bench, brushed her fingers against my crotch. I swatted them away.

"You're just a coward," she said.

"You wouldn't even understand," I said. Suddenly, my dreamy recollection of last night came into focus, clean, whole. And I felt an anger surging through all my aches and pains.

Beth licked her lips and said, "You don't know what you're missing."

Chapter Thirty-one

I swerved the big truck off the highway and we landed loudly onto the gravel of the shoulder. I slammed the gearshift into park.

"What's your problem?" Beth demanded.

"You," I said, jerking open the driver's door. A cold blast flooded the cab. "Get out." I reached across and grabbed her arm. I pulled her roughly across the console and out my door. She was light and surprised, otherwise I might not have been able to get her. Every muscle in my body screamed in pain. I slammed the door shut and pushed her against the side of the Suburban.

"You're nuts!" she shrieked, trying to back away from me. I hemmed her in with both my arms.

"You've been lying to me since the first time I saw you," I shouted above the wind.

"No!" she shouted back, trying to duck under my arms. I slammed my fist into the side of the truck, just beside her head. It got her attention.

"You lied about not talking to Leo. You lied about Camelback Falls. You lied about that night in Guadalupe."

"I lied to save my life!"

"Dave…" It was Lindsey. She came around the back of the truck, having climbed out the other side.

Beth glanced at Lindsey. "He's just putting on a show for you because I offered to suck his cock," she said. Then, back to me: "Calm down, big fella."

"No more bullshit, Beth," I said, leaning in to her face. She turned away.

I said, "You told us you watched a deputy take cocaine out of a patrol car."

"I did," she yelled. The wind pushed her hair straight back from her forehead. I could see intricate canals of worry wrinkles running horizontally in her pale skin.

"The car that was driven by Matson and Bullock."

"Yes!"

"Where were you sitting?" I demanded.

"In the squad car! They put me there."

"Where was the car?"

She hesitated. Two patches of dark crescents emerged under her eyes. Finally, "It was parked right there, where I could see…"

"That's bullshit, Beth! You were in Nixon's patrol car, and that was parked out on the street, not in the alley where you could see Matson and Bullock's car. You didn't see Peralta take the coke."

Beth shouted, "You don't know what you're talking about. I'm telling the truth. I saw it. I was there."

"I was there, too, Beth."

She stared at me, a wild look on her face. The wind was so cold, my eyes felt like they were drying out. An ancient car full of Indians slowed to see if we needed help. Lindsey waved them on.

"No!" Beth shouted.

"Yes. I was a young deputy. Before I left to teach. I'm the one who handcuffed you. I stuck you in a patrol car where you couldn't have seen anything."

She thumped me hard on the chest, and crumpled backward onto the side of the truck. "You bastard," she sobbed. "You tricked me, you son of a bitch."

"You didn't see any of that, did you, Beth." I persisted. I grabbed her and shook her. She felt like a rag doll in my arms. "Tell me the damned truth!"

I pushed her away. She bent over, hands on her knees, breathing heavily and sobbing. I signaled to Lindsey, and opened the driver's door.

"What are you doing?" Beth screamed.

"Leaving you," I said. "You're no good to me as a witness. I'll tell the tribal police you need a ride."

I closed the door. Lindsey climbed in the passenger side. I slid the Suburban into drive. Lindsey said quietly, "Cocksuck your way back to Denver, baby."

Beth pounded on the driver's window. "Don't leave me!"

I started rolling forward slowly.

"Bastard!" She hit the window hard. "They told me to tell that story!"

I stepped on the brake and lowered the window two inches.

"They told me, if anybody ever asked, to say a deputy named Peralta stole that cocaine," she said, breathless. "They told me again last week to say the same thing. They said he was the sheriff now. They said they'd kill me if I didn't."

I lowered the window halfway, my finger on the remote-control button like it was a torture device.

"Who is they?"

"The detective! I don't know." Her fingers were red and raw from the cold, clutching the top of the window.

"Who is they, damn it!" I let the truck start to roll.

She screamed a name. I felt a new chill.

"I want to know what those goons were after," I pushed.

"You were there," she said. "You heard. They wanted to know where Leo was."

"That's right," I said into the wind. "I was there. I heard them say 'Give it up.' Not 'Give him up,' but 'Give it up.' What is it, Beth?"

"How would I know? This is insane!"

I let up the brake and the truck rolled. The highway was empty to the horizon in both directions. "No!" she yelled and sobbed. "Don't leave me!"

"The truth, Beth."

"They wanted the letter."

I put the truck into park.

"Dean Nixon wrote me a letter six weeks ago. How he found me after all these years, I don't know. He and Leo had been in contact, and he said he wanted to make things right for Leo. I guess he wanted to do one good thing before his life was over. He said he was going to tell what really happened in Gaudalupe, what really happened with the cocaine. He was going to go to the new sheriff, Peralta. But he was afraid. And he was afraid for what might happen to Leo. The River Hogs had gang contacts inside the prison, and they could kill him if he seemed like he was going to talk."

"Where's the letter, Beth?"

She looked at me, red-eyed, and more tears came down her cheeks. She reached into her pants and pulled out a folded piece of paper. She handed it to me carefully, and I handed it to Lindsey. I stepped out to open the back door for her. She fell back against the side of the truck and said, "I'm so tired of this."

"Get in, Beth."

"You may as well know, things that night didn't go down the way I said."

I faced her. She looked wrung out, her skin bloodless.

"We were going to rob those old cops. Me and Billy and Troyce. We were going to double-cross Dean. We had Jonathan's money, and the cops had the stolen drugs, and we were going to take both. Jonathan wouldn't miss it, and Billy and Troyce wanted to go to Mexico. Poor Leo was just along because he loved me."

"What are you saying?"

"I'm saying, when those deputies, Matson and Bullock, pulled in behind us that night, they thought they were just going to get cash for the drugs they took from the evidence room. I got out of the car..."

Her words sunk in. I suddenly said, "Beth, anything you say—" She held out a hand in a violent "stop" gesture. "Don't read me my fucking rights. I got out of the car and walked back and smiled, and they were just stupid fucking men."

"Anything you say can and will be used against you in a court of law."

"I know that," she said. "I also know I have a right to counsel. Just like Leo did." She sobbed and rubbed her nose. "I waive my rights. Don't you get it, Mapstone? While I distracted those old guys, Billy and Troyce got out of the car and came up and shot them. Right there. It happened so fast. Then, they started going through their pants to get the car keys, to get the coke out of the trunk. But it was too late. You guys charged in. I guess Nixon finally got the coke. Maybe the detective did. I don't know." She shook her head against the implacable wind. Then she shouted, "So, you see, I've had a lot to try to run away from all these years."

"You didn't know they were going to kill those cops," I blurted suddenly, inappropriately chivalrous.

She looked at me, a look like the young girl Marybeth had in that vivid photo from Camelback Falls.

She said, "Yes, I did."

Chapter Thirty-two

We delivered Beth to the huge, glassy Sandra Day O'Connor Federal Building in downtown Phoenix. To me, it still looked like a call center in the suburbs. Inside, we sat through hours of interviews with the U.S. Attorney's staff, through a magnificent Arizona sunset out the big windows, and then Beth went off into protective custody with two marshals. What I really wanted was a shower, a drink, and a long sleep with Lindsey curled up against me.

"Sheriff!"

It was Kimbrough, waiting at the foot of the escalator as we descended into the enormous glass shell of the atrium. He shook my hand, then gave Lindsey an awkward hug.

"Congratulations," he said, "We're not waiting for federal indictments, either. We've already picked up two of these bounty hunters. And they've given up two other scumbags, former deputies, who were working with them. And we have arrest warrants issued for all the ones you said on the phone."

He looked at my face. "Man, that must hurt," he said. It did. It looked worse. On a trip to the men's room, I spent several minutes scrutinizing the colors of my shiner.

"Don't ask about Peralta," he said. "I don't know anything new." We walked past the metal detectors and out onto Washington Street. Outside, it was nicely brisk—balmy compared to the weather in Denver or out on the Navajo Reservation with Beth by the roadside.

"You know Beth cleared him," I said.

He bit his lip. "I know she backed away from saying he stole that cocaine." We stopped on the street, facing each other. "Look, don't make me the bad guy in this, Sheriff. I'm just doing the job. We still have to deal with Peralta's badge number in Nixon's payoff book."

"Maybe we don't," Lindsey said. A little clot of traffic passed by, and she went on.

"While Dave was getting beaten up, I took all the badge numbers in the book and set up a database to handle other information we had about East County deputies for April, May, and June 1979. Things like personal logs, court appearances, overtime reports, sick time. Then I created a program to make some comparisons.

"Here's the thing: It doesn't make any sense the way Nixon recorded it. He lists a payoff of $1,200 to Peralta's badge number on April 3, but for most of that month Peralta was at an FBI school in Quantico."

I remembered. He was.

"The same result comes out in several other instances. A payoff is given to a badge number, but the deputy is on sick leave. Another payoff is listed, but that badge number goes to somebody who's been transferred to the West Valley."

"So," Kimbrough said, "you're saying it's all bogus?"

"Not necessarily," Lindsey said. "It might be pretty simple. They might have thrown in some innocent deputies on that list to provide cover, just in case they were ever caught. Or it might be a code. For example, maybe Peralta's badge number in the logbook actually means somebody else. I ran some scenarios that way, and they came out in a way that would make sense. Maybe not airtight for a courtroom, but enough to point us to the real dirty cops. Certainly enough to clear Peralta."

"Wait a damned minute," Kimbrough said. "I want this to be a happy ending, too. But you're using technology that didn't even exist twenty years ago, and if it did no damned sheriff's deputy knew how to use it."

"They wouldn't have to," I said. "It would be as simple as a sheet of paper with the real dirty cops and their badge numbers on one side, and the decoy badge numbers on the other. Just a simple key. Now I don't know why that key wasn't with Nixon's book. But the bad guys obviously thought we had it."

Kimbrough stuck his hands in his pockets and stared at the sidewalk. "OK, Sheriff," he said. "Maybe it gives us a starting point."

I leaned over and whispered to Lindsey, "You're pretty smart for a propellerhead." She lightly stroked my cheek.

"Sheriff Mapstone!"

It was a federal guard, walking briskly from the building. "You got a message. It came through the security office. From a woman named Sharon at Good Samaritan?"

"Yeah?" I felt a cold bolt driven into my legs.

"She wants you at the hospital. Said it's urgent. Does that make sense?"

"I guess so," I heard myself say.

"Here," Kimbrough pointed us toward the curb. "We can take my car."

〈 〉〈 〉〈 〉

The elevator moved upstairs slowly. It was sized for two or three hospital beds, but the three of us just seemed to move involuntarily into one corner. The cables and gears churned quietly. The panel glowed with a single button depressed to the correct floor. And then we were there. The doors opened with a heavy jerk. I forced myself to walk quickly down the hall, half-lit now for night running. Across the polished floor tiles: Step on a crack…My stomach felt that hard thumb of pain again. My panic attack, if Beth was to be believed. To have come through all this just to…

"Mapstone."

Peralta lay in his bed, halfway raised, his large dark eyes wonderfully open. His skin was too pale and his lips were badly chapped. But he looked at us. We bunched up in the doorway, afraid to walk farther.

"Mapstone," he repeated, his voice reedy and soft. "Where the hell have you been?"

Sharon was sitting in a chair beside the head of the bed. She looked up at us and began to tear up. "He woke up two hours ago. Just woke up." She swallowed hard. "I'm taught to discount miracles. I'll take this one."

I stepped forward and put a hand on his big shoulder. "Good to have you back," I said.

He shook his head. "You got beat up, Mapstone."

"I hurt 'em back," I said.

His eyes followed me. "Did you get the bad guys?" he asked.

"Almost," I said. "We're about to get them all."

"You know about Camelback Falls, the River Hogs?" he whispered insistently.

"David, let him rest. . ." Sharon prodded.

I pleaded with her with my eyes. I glanced back at Kimbrough, then Lindsey. Then I pulled up a chair and let him talk.

He filled in some gaps for us. Told us what we needed to know. I could hear Kimbrough scratching some notes on his pad.

Peralta closed his eyes for a second, then gave in to some coughing—also a wonderful relief to hear. He looked at me again, and this time his voice had some of the old steel in it.

"Well," he said. "Don't get too used to that title, Sheriff Mapstone."

I smiled so wide my face convulsed in a dozen points of pain. It felt great.

Chapter Thirty-three

I watched the sunset that night, a prisoner of the glass of the federal building, and it was a tragedy. It had rained while we were in Denver and then cleared. The sky was scrubbed clean. The twilight spreading out from the west deserved the full wonder that came from standing in endless space and breathing wild dry Western air. But the view through the window would do. At least once a month, Lindsey and I tried to take in a sunset from the Compass Room at the top of the Hyatt, just to remind ourselves that for all of Phoenix's flaws, we lived in a place of daily miracles.

It was already full dark when Kimbrough delivered us to Cypress Street. Off on Seventh Avenue, some moron was gunning his car, trying to find someone to impress. But Willo was dark, quiet, and safe. The house was safe. The cat was glad to see us. And a note was sandwiched in the windshield wiper of Lindsey's Prelude.

That's why an hour later I turned off Camelback Road onto Arcadia Lane and followed the street as it wound its way up the mountain. I parked in a dirt turnoff, shut off the lights, and stepped out. The night was cool and dry, magical in the way that only 14 percent humidity can do. Around me at discreet distances, multi-million-dollar homes sparkled like miniature galaxies glimpsed through enchanted telescopes. I'd never own one of those houses on a professor's paycheck, much less on a deputy sheriff's.

Jonathan Ledger had done all right. His glass-and-marble dream-house still clung to the side of the mountain. Some ornamental lights marked off the gate and the path down to the house, but otherwise the place looked like it hadn't been lived in since Reagan was president. A Realtor's sign. Another sign warned of alarms. I thought of Yeats' poem, but ignored the sign. I lifted a heavy iron latch on the gate, swung it open, and stepped inside.

Past the gate, the mountainside desert encased me in silence. The path was paved and led downhill at a steep angle. I walked as silently as I could, past some overgrown stands of jumping cactus and creosote bush. Civilization was never far away: breaking the surface of the sandy soil were some metal conduits, leading down to the house.

The place was bigger than it looked from the road. It hugged the side of the mountain and cascaded down in two levels. Rock-encrusted walls disappeared into Camelback's soil. An interior courtyard was guarded by a black, wrought-iron gate. Around on the side facing the city, I got a sense of the place. It was mostly glass, framed by stone and what looked like redwood timbers. It was dark inside—the owners were who-knows-where in the global economy. But I swore I could make out the smooth surfaces of the interior fountain, Camelback Falls.

"I didn't think you'd come."

The voice came from behind me, and then a figure stepped out onto a flat promontory beside the glassed wall. He was small and slender. I could just make out the light reflected in his eyes.

The voice continued, a pleasant tenor without an accent. "That night, when I called you. I was sure everything was ruined, and you'd think I shot the sheriff and was trying to kill you."

"What really happened?" I asked. I felt as if I had stumbled upon the unicorn. I was afraid to step forward.

"I had to get out," he said. "I had to try to escape. They would have killed me otherwise. Nixon got word to me that I was going to be killed. I didn't have a choice. Have you talked to Nixon?"

"He's dead," I said. I felt a touch of vertigo, standing on the slope, a nice slide of 1,000 feet through rock and cactus just a step away. I saw Dean Nixon's face so clearly. But it was the face of a nineteen-year-old, stupid and hopeful and untouched by the world.

The figure came closer. Leo O'Keefe shook his head and said, "Oh, dear God, will this never end?"

He looked over his shoulder at the city lights, then back at me. "Nixon contacted me six months ago. He wanted to go to Chief Peralta, tell what really happened in Guadalupe. How the cops were on the take, how they stole the drugs. How those convicts were really in with them."

"Why did he have a change of heart?"

"I don't know," he said. "He said he'd fallen in love with a woman, she was a Christian, and he'd been doing a lot of thinking about his past. About what the River Hogs did to me. Whatever the reason, he came out to the prison, and we met several times. He wanted to help me make a case for a pardon from the governor. But somebody found out in the Sheriff's Office, and Dean got scared."

"Twenty-one years ago," I said. "Did someone talk to you after you were arrested? Somebody who told you what to say?"

"God, yes," he said, and named the name.

"That's what Beth said. She's come back from Denver to testify."

Leo shook his head. "I always forget she's changed her name," he said. "It makes her mad when I call her Marybeth."

"But you killed a man, Leo. We can't undo that."

His body language was calm. He just stood there, a figure in half-darkness, rooted to the mountainside. He said, "I know that. Does it make any difference that he tried to kill me? He was sent by the River Hogs to take me out. They didn't trust me to shut up. But I used to work in the peanut mills, in the summers, back in Oklahoma. Hauling around those bags. I was stronger than I looked. He made a stupid move, and I let him fall on his knife."

"I hadn't heard that."

"I've only been trying to tell it for twenty years."

That was the last sound I heard before the gunbarrel exploded.

A flash came from the direction of my left shoulder, and Leo was lifted off the ground and deposited in the rocks five feet away. My first instinct was to hit the ground. My second was to run to the little man who sprawled unnaturally on his back. Neither move was particularly smart. But there I was, kneeling before Leo O'Keefe. He looked like a broken mannequin. A dark liquid trailed out the side of his mouth. In the reflected light I could see deep creases cut into his face, and how his ponytail was gray. He was younger than me. I cradled his shoulders helplessly, letting the burrs and rocks cut into my knees. He stared up at me and tried to speak.

"Nice job, Sheriff. You got your man."

I stayed on my knees, trying to keep Leo's airway open. But I could clearly see a face when I turned toward the house.

"Too bad you'll be fatally wounded in the capture," Bill Davidson said.

In the light reflected from the city he still looked like the Marlboro man. Tall, slender, rugged—getting more handsome every year he got older. He wore a Western-cut white shirt and nicely aged denim. In his right hand was the blued barrel of a revolver. In his left was a semiautomatic.

"So that's how it still works?" I said. "Do what you want. Plant the evidence to back it up."

He shrugged. "There's nobody to blame for this but David Mapstone," he said. "You could have stopped this at any time. God, I made you sheriff. And that damned idiot Abernathy went along with it. But, yeah, that's how things play out now. I shot O'Keefe with this weapon." He hefted the semiautomatic. "And I'll leave that with you. I'll shoot you with this revolver, which I'll leave with Leo." His teeth shone in the light. "You'll have a grand funeral, Sheriff."

I said, "Nobody will believe it. I'd never carry a semiautomatic." That seemed to throw him off stride, but he moved closer. My Python was in my belt, an impossible six inches away from my right hand. I stood slowly.

"Don't you fucking move!" he ordered, his deep voice quavering. "Why couldn't you let this go? This was nothing to you."

"Just that someone tried to murder my friend." The Python weighed heavily on my waist.

"He could have let it go, too," Davidson said. "Peralta didn't have to reopen this. That scumbag Nixon stirred it all up again."

"The past has a way of coming around," I said. "Like that night in Guadalupe. You told me you were off duty, with a sick child. What you didn't tell me was that you came downtown later, plainclothes, to threaten Beth and Leo to lie about the dirty cops they saw."

"Dirty cops," he snorted. "Do you know what a joke you were as a cop, Mapstone?"

"I never rated the River Hogs," I said.

"Damned straight," he said, without irony. "We kept the fucking peace out in the county. I never took a vow of poverty."

"It was that simple?"

"Let me tell you something, it was the simplest thing in the world. One night, Nixon and I were working undercover. We busted these two scumbag drug dealers out in Apache Junction. They've got like a trunkful of pot in their trailer. And the phone rings. It was one of their fucking customers. Nixon and I just looked at each other, and we knew what we were going to do. We didn't bust them. We sold them the drugs."

"And that was the River Hogs?"

"That was my River Hogs," Davidson said. "The bunch of guys who went drinking down in the riverbed off duty, they might get a piece of the action if they could be trusted. If they got it."

"Like Matson and Bullock got it," I said.

"They were idiots," Davidson said. "Nixon let 'em in. Not me. But I had to come in and clean it up in the end." He waved the semiautomatic at me. "Nixon was nuts. He was high half the time. He was off playing stud at that rich doctor's sex parties."

"What about Peralta? How'd you buy him off?"

Davidson laughed like an executioner who liked his work. "Peralta wouldn't be bought. The son-of-a-bitch. I offered him a stake. He threw it in my face. So I made sure we recorded his badge number when we were handing out the bonuses, just in case he decided to take it to Internal Affairs."

"He didn't?"

"How the hell should I know? After the shooting, everything changed. We stopped the parties. Nixon and I kept running a few scams, just for pocket change. But I shut up those two kids. Peralta was off climbing the ladder. Everything would have been fine if that fuck Dick Nixon hadn't decided, twenty years later, to grow a conscience."

"It's a bitch when that happens," I said quietly. "And if you have to ruin the lives of two kids…"

"I can't solve all the problems in the world," he said. "I have to look after me and my own. You expect me to do it on a deputy's paycheck?" He waved one of the guns at the lights of the mansions on the mountainside. "Look at these fuckers, living this way. They do it because we protect their asses from the bad guys. Protect and serve."

"Davidson, you're one of the bad guys."

"Goodbye, Sheriff," he said. "You understand why I've got to end this here."

"Don't move!" A shout from below.

They looked like mutant fireflies, those little red laser beams on Davidson's chest. He looked down at them calmly.

"Don't move a fucking muscle!" Kimbrough shouted, easing himself up the ridge, his gun drawn. "We've got SWAT snipers who will take you out before you even inhale!" The red lightning bugs wiggled on Davidson's chest. It was the distraction I needed to pull out my big Colt.

Davidson's handsome, lined face broke into a crazy smile. "Shit," he said, waving his arms dreamily, holding out the pistols. "I captured an escaped convict! That's Leo O'Keefe, right there. He shot Peralta. He was going to shoot the sheriff here. I stopped him."

Kimbrough was at my side, his dark Glock leveled at Davidson's chest. Davidson started toward us, then stopped. We held our ground. Davidson seemed suddenly disoriented. He looked at the lasers on his chest, then glanced out at the city.

"I'm going to be the chief deputy," he said, tears running down his rugged face. "Shit."

Suddenly a low roar came over the mountain and descended toward us, then it turned into a bone-rattling windstorm and we were lit up like judgment day. Davidson stared at the helicopter, fifty feet above us. I stepped forward and hammered him under his chin, dropping him to the ground. I grabbed the revolver and Kimbrough wrestled away the semiautomatic. He looked at us as if he were awakening from a dream.

"You've got to kill me, Mapstone," he yelled, his face death-white in the spotlight of the chopper. "You can't send a cop to prison." He reached for my gun. "Goddamn it! You owe me that!"

I pushed him back down and stepped back. Then I felt the dark shapes of the SWAT officers swarming around us. One of them roughly handcuffed Davidson and hauled him to his feet.

"Take him to jail," I said.

A long convoy of emergency vehicles trickled back down the mountain. The chopper sailed off toward downtown. I sat off to myself and watched, a solitary figure on a cold, dark boulder. Behind me, the house was dark. The ghosts of Jonathan Ledger and Dean Nixon watched us in worldly silence. When I felt a hand on my shoulder, I was shivering from the cold.

"History Shamus, I'm here to take you home."

I just sat and shook my head. Lindsey came down close and wrapped her arms around me.

"We have 'Protect and Serve' written on our cars," I said. "We didn't do that with Leo, now did we?"

"You did the best you could, Dave," she said.

"Not good enough."

She whispered, "Oh, baby. Come home now."

She sat beside me, and for long time I just savored her warmth and softness as counterpoint to the rock beneath me. Then we stood up and I brushed away her dark hair, ran my finger down her cheekbone. Her eyes were full of tears, and then mine were, too. I didn't know why I was blessed enough to be loved in a cold, deadly world where everything was at risk.

"What happened?" I gently touched the empty skin of her nostril, where the nose stud used to be. "Are you going back in uniformed duty?"

She shook her head and smiled. "Oh, Dave. The world turns around. Life goes on." She held up her hand. The engagement ring sparkled. "This is the jewel I need in my life now."

I kissed her lightly and slipped my hand around her waist, so familiar and so wondrous. We stood in the darkness of the mountainside, alone now. The great desert city spread out at our feet, vast and charmed and cursed, destiny and history, a billion electric diamonds, shimmering with possibilities.

To receive a free catalog of Poisoned Pen Press titles, please
contact us in one of the following ways:

Phone: 1-800-421-3976
Facsimile: 1-480-949-1707
Email: info@poisonedpenpress.com
Website: www.poisonedpenpress.com

Poisoned Pen Press
6962 E. First Ave. Ste. 103
Scottsdale, AZ 85251